My Lucky Star

My Lucky Star

Texas Hill Country
1846

Susan Thomas

Illustrated by

Katherine Gaile Jacobs

My Lucky Star

Susan Thomas
New Braunfels, Texas 78130

Susanthomasbooks.com
susan@susanthomasbooks

ISBN:979-8-218-51781-6

For all the brave and courageous children in my life, especially those with dyslexia. Your courage and grit are an inspiration.

Author's Note

As I sit, writing this book, on my comfortable couch, sipping hot tea made in an electric kettle, and contemplating turning up the air conditioner, I can't help but think about my ancestors and the hardships they faced to start a new life here in Texas. I love my state with its rich history and its wide-open spaces and am so grateful that somewhere along the line, so many of my relatives decided Texas was where they wanted to be.

This book is my attempt to bring their stories to life and to help children everywhere have an appreciation for their own as well as our collective past. We do not fully know who we are without knowing where we came from.

Even if you don't know your own family's history, or if your history is one you'd rather forget, there is always value in knowing who walked in these places before you. Their stories are a part of us all.

Of note – when writing this book, in order to relate realistic dialogue, I use the terminology the German immigrants used for Native Americans as seen in firsthand accounts. These terms include 'Indians' and 'Wild Ones'. Both are generic terms used for all Native Americans by the German immigrants in the 1800's.

My great grandparents, Arwed Hillmann and Christine Seipp Hillmann, along with my grandfather (far right) Helwig Hillman. Also shown is a great aunt.

Part 1

April 23, 1846
New Braunfels, Texas

"Courage is the commitment to begin without any guarantee of success"
~ Johann Wolfgang von Goethe

1

A New Adventure

"Hurry Mama, I don't want to be late!" eleven-year-old Anna Schupp blurted as a flutter of excitement rolled around in her stomach. Mama gave a "hmmmf" as she finished braiding Anna's long blonde hair. Twisting her skirts in her hands, Anna went on, "They'll leave us. I know they will if we're not there on time. Papa said so. The carts won't wait and we'll have to catch up."

Her brother, Henry, sat on a nearby bench on the porch of the cabin they had been staying in while they prepared for the next leg of their journey, beating his boots together. "Bye Anna," he teased as he slipped on one well-worn dusty boot, "We'll see you in Fredericksburg. Good luck with the Indians along the way."

Anna simply raised her eyebrows and replied, "I think I spotted a scorpion in one of your boots last night. It might still be in there...." She was rewarded by a quick flash of concern on Henry's face, but then he smiled and shrugged his shoulders, pulling on his other boot and stretching in the morning sun. "Don't worry, little sister, I won't let the wagons leave. I'll lie down on the road in front of them if I have to," Henry declared, puffing out his chest and standing tall.

"Henrich Schupp, you'd be little more than a bump in the road to those oxen. They'd think you were a rock. Well

... you do have rocks in your head," Anna needled her brother.

Mama, taking a deep breath, interrupted, "Enough, you two, please ... *please* help me with these bundles. You make me tired just listening to you."

Anna and Henry exchanged a look. Mama was always tired nowadays, since arriving on the Texas coast....

"Mama, do you think I'll have time to stop and see Elizabeth one last time before we leave? I promise I won't stay long. I just ..." Anna pleaded suddenly.

"Anna, you said your goodbyes," Mama sighed. "You'll see your friend in Fredericksburg in a few months, as soon as she's well enough to travel again. You just said yourself we can't be late. I know you'll miss her, but don't worry. She's out of danger now."

Mama closed her eyes and pressed two fingers in the crease

between her delicate brows. She took a deep breath and continued, "I don't know how she survived, but she did, praise be."

"Yes, she did!" Anna whooped, "And it was because of you, Mama; you kept her alive. I was so afraid she would die in Karlshafen. It was awful enough living in that sandy cave on the beach full of horrible bugs, but when cholera started creeping through the camp, I thought we were all going to die."

Mama replied, "I think it was you who pulled her through, Anna. You and your lucky star."

As they did so often, the memories of those awful weeks in Karlshafen, the port of Indianola on the Texas coast, flashed quickly through Anna's mind, and she remembered the strain on Mama's face – the exhaustion of each and every step she took. Anna remembered praying and distracting her friend from her misery by looking at the stars in the night sky and declaring, "Elizabeth, look at that big one. That's YOUR lucky star, just like the one on the Texas flag we saw when we first arrived. God put it there just for you! You can't die tonight ... your lucky star won't let you!"

"And the wagons!" Henry chimed in, interrupting her thoughts. "We finally got wagons after all those months. I would have built one myself if Mr. Meusebach hadn't found a way to wrangle some away from the War with Mexico. What rotten luck – to arrive just when war broke out. Too bad there weren't any spare guns. I want to learn to shoot!"

"Ha! You ... with a gun?" Anna scoffed with a wide-eyed, exaggerated shudder that caused Henry to smirk at his sister.

"You just wait, baby sister, I'll shoot as well as anyone," Henry retorted. "I bet you wished a gun was by my side all those nights we were sleeping in the open on our trek across the lowlands. I noticed you scooting closer every time you heard a coyote or the crunch of dead leaves nearby ... but *silences* are the worst because when a predator is nearby, the animals that go silent are the ones more likely to live. Goes to show what YOU know about danger! Ja* I bet you wished I had a gun next to me on those nights."

Anna sniffed, "I did not wish any such thing. I was just too tired to know what I was doing. Being bumped and

Ja – German for 'Yes'

battered all day long in the wagon wasn't exactly restful, but I wasn't too eager to step on a snake or get wet boots either."

Then, noticing Mama's sad eyes, she admitted, "But we really do need to get going. It won't be so bad this time, I'm sure."

Looking around and lost in thought, Mama lamented, leaning heavily on the porch railing, "Oh you two ... you have to admit New Braunfels is a really nice place. Maybe we should just stay here. The rivers are so clear and beautiful and so cold – they remind me of home."

Then she dropped her head in her hands and moaned, "Oh, why can't we just stay here?"

Anna glanced meaningfully at her brother. "You're right, Mama. Yesterday I watched the springs where the Comal bubbles right up out of the rocks and flows into pools. Papa explained it's a sacred place for the Indians. It was so beautiful … When we got here, I thought I'd gone to heaven." Anna gently continued, "… but we can't stay here. You know that. For one thing, the carts are already loaded." With her determination growing, Anna set her jaw and declared, "Mama, our new home is going to be Fredericksburg. Let's go."

Encouraged by Anna's strength, Mama straightened and brushed a stray wisp of hair out of her eyes.

Henry added helpfully, "Papa says all beginnings are hard. Fredericksburg will grow too one day and be a way station just like this one … for travelers to the grant area. Don't worry, Mama, we'll help you."

With that, they all took a deep breath and were gathering their last bundles when they noticed Papa walking down the road with purpose.

"Oh William ... William Schupp!" Mama called, gathering all her resolve and waving from the front porch as he passed on his way to the Sophienburg, the gathering place and headquarters for the Immigration Society on the top of the hill, "Don't forget to leave room for the eggs!"

"Yes Christine, yes, I remember. I'll not forget your eggs," he replied with a weary smile. Papa was busy, as usual, taking care of everything they needed to survive.

She was grateful for it, but she missed the times he used to tell them the Grimm Brothers Fairy Tales. He knew lots of them, but Little Red Riding Hood and Hansel and Gretel were her favorites. She missed more of Papa than just stories. She missed his smiles and laughter too.

Papa hurried by and Henry started for the porch stairs, intending to catch up with him. As he passed her, he gave a yank on Anna's braid.

"Ohoo oh! I'll get you, Henry," she cried, swatting at him and narrowly missing. "If Mama hadn't been in the way, I'd have you for sure!" she called after him.

They used to play this game all the time. If Anna was quick enough to tag him, he would bow, recognizing her quickness with a wink and a smile. She watched Henry run after Papa and thought of how they didn't play much of anything since the ship left the port in Bremen, Germany. Onboard, there was time to play games, as long as they stayed out of the way, and Papa told stories to pass the time. Since then, there was only enough energy for survival – and watching for the constant threat of danger.

Anna was glad to see her brother playing again. Were easier times ahead? The weather was warmer, and most of the April showers were gone. The fields around the town of New Braunfels were bursting with colors of blue, yellow, and red as spring grasses and fresh flowers found every patch of soil to cling to, whether it was on a rocky outcropping over the river, or in the large fields surrounding the east side of town.

Mama gave Anna a small nudge and drew in a deep breath, "OK Anna, we're ready. Help me with these last things."

"Yes, Mama," Anna replied, "Don't worry. This adventure will be a good one. You'll see."

"Oh Anna, I hope you're right. All of life is an adventure for you! You're never afraid of anything or anyone. You have faith, always faith. It's just …" Mama trailed away, not finishing her thought.

Anna knew what that thought was. It was the Indians.

They left Germany looking for opportunity and a better life, selling all their worldly belongings to join the Society for the Protection of German Immigrants in Texas, or "The Society" as Papa called it for short. Now they were here, with many other Germans, all fleeing the hardships of Germany. All headed to the wilderness of the Texas frontier. They came with the promises from The Society for land that was in their words, "abundant with water, timber, and grass."

It was just that there was the small problem of Comanche Indians.

Anna shuddered to remember the faces of the Americans they passed along the way; the way they shook their heads and muttered. Interpreting for her, their driver remarked, "They are saying, 'Better you than me.'" After that, Anna always kept her head up and her eyes forward as she passed them, thinking, "Yes, it is better *me* than *you*. I will succeed. You would not."

2

Saying Goodbye

"Auf Wiedersehen, we are all so very grateful," Anna smiled as she gave the Lindemann family hugs. "Your cabin was perfect after months sleeping in the open."

Having arrived a year earlier, the Lindemanns remembered well the hardships of travel and willingly added more straw filled pallets on the floor for the newcomers.

"Auf Wiedersehen - a German expression meaning "until we meet again" or "goodbye"

Anna delighted in the nights spent laying side by side. She preferred the sounds of so many people sleeping close over those of the open fields. Here, with the grunts and snores of men and the burrowing of the children into their covers, she slept better than she could remember for months.

The house was small, just one room with a chimney on one end, and made of rough logs with canvas from wagons stretched over the top for a roof. There was a porch that faced the

river and one that faced the road as well. The sloping hill that led to the Comal River was the perfect spot to roll and play with the other children, pick wildflowers, and rest in the warm afternoon sun for the past few weeks.

Anna turned and started up the hill towards the headquarters, looking back at the river one last time. Cypress, pecan, and oak trees hugged its banks. She paused and listened to the musical flow of the passing water. It seemed to speak to her and tell her Texas was not so forbidding after all. She thought of the days ahead and remembered her last journey. She remembered the forever days of walking or riding through the boggy lowlands and endless fields of prairie grass as high as her waist. She remembered the feelings of never being clean and always being hungry.

Thinking of her empty stomach, she asked, "Mama, will we have eggs for supper on the road? I hope so! Oh, how I love fresh eggs!"

"Nein* Anna, our eggs will be hatched by the brood hens. We'll make a small coop to protect them and hopefully keep them alive long enough to hatch. Planning ahead will put food on the table, and we'll have to be resourceful. There will be times of need ahead for us," Mama explained, hurrying her step. "That stomach of yours is always hungry. With two growing children, we will need food and lots of it."

Anna set her pace to match Mama's, looking ahead for the wagons. Walking quickly past the tall steeple of the German Protestant Church, she panted, "Mama, look at that beautiful
*Nein - German for "No"

19

church – the dome on top looks like a pastry puff. Think of the fine work those men did in building it – and in only a year! We will do the same. We'll build homes, churches, and stores in no time. You wait and see."

Mama nodded her head in hopeful agreement, but stayed silent as they trudged up the road, arms full of last-minute bundles.

As they approached the long log building that was the headquarters of The Society, Henry came running toward them. "The carts are ready and the oxen are hitched! The eggs are settled and safe, Mama, I checked myself. We are just waiting for the signal to move out. They say we'll be going slow, marking the route for the next group." Bouncing on his toes, he added, "Just think, Anna, we will be the first children, well other than Indians, to walk down these rocky trails into the wild ... you wanted adventure ... now you will get it!"

Anna looked skeptically at the two-wheeled Mexican carts holding their supplies of beans, flour, bacon, and the like, as well as their trunks. She blurted, "I hope these things are sturdier than they look! I don't want the adventure of *carrying* our things all the way to Fredericksburg ..."

Anna turned to look back over the town and was surprised to see Elizabeth hurrying towards her. Running to her friend, Anna hugged her tightly. "Oh Elizabeth, you are a sight! You shouldn't be out of bed. You need your rest and you know it," Anna admonished. Shaking her finger, she couldn't help but smile at her friend. Trying to sound motherly, she continued, "And you are too pale, and you look ready to drop."

Holding onto her friend for support, Elizabeth sighed, "Oh Anna, I just couldn't miss saying goodbye. I'll miss you so much!"

"We will see each other again soon." Anna encouraged, "It will be wonderful in Fredericksburg when you arrive. We will sit out at night and look at the stars again. When you miss me, find your lucky star and know that God is with us both."

Anna continued hopefully, "And look how much nicer it is here than on the coast. Almost no mosquitos!" Anna laughed. "Remember how awful those beasts were? Who would have thought such a small thing could cause so much grief. Hundreds of them were always swarming, even in my ears and nose! I'll take Indians over mosquitos any day!"

Elizabeth replied, "I'm sure you would, Anna Schupp, but be careful what you wish for."

Growing serious, Anna replied, "Mama wishes for the comfort of a house and a bed, Papa wishes for a new start, and Henry wishes to be a man and shoot guns. What do *I* wish for? I don't have the luxury of wishing. Wishing doesn't make things happen. Doing makes them happen. Wishes only set you up for disappointment. You *will* come to Fredericksburg in a few months, Elizabeth. We will have a house for you to stay in, and we will not give in to this wild place or the Indians. Do you hear me?"

"You are my steadfast friend, Anna," Elizabeth replied, "My strong, steadfast friend. Your faith in the future somehow makes everything seem possible. What would I have done without you all those miles telling me that I could do it and entertaining me with stories?"

"Well, I'll have lots more of those for you once you get to Fredericksburg," Anna breathed, relaxing a little, "So don't even think about staying here!"

As the guide called for the oxen to move out, Anna quickly gave Elizabeth one last hug and ran to her family's cart in the middle of the line.

Anna called, "See you in a few months, Elizabeth Lehmann. Get in bed and get strong!"

3

The Journey Begins

The two wheeled ox carts pulled out of New Braunfels on April 23, 1846. Now, only two days later, Anna and Henry were exhausted. They worked harder than they ever imagined, moving heavy stones so the carts, packed with all the household belongings in heavy wooden trunks, could cross the shallow rivers and make their way along uneven, rocky trails. All day they worked, along with anyone else who was strong enough, to drive one wedge after another under the rocks to build makeshift bridges and fill in deep ruts along the trail.

As they headed northwest, away from New Braunfels, the ground quickly shifted from grassy, rolling hills, to rough, rocky terrain intermixed with thick patches of live oak trees, their twisted arms open wide and hanging low. Patches of grass and flowers were everywhere, and the limestone rocks, trees, and grassy fields seemed to be old friends who enjoyed each other's company.

When not moving rocks, Anna walked along with the carts, getting to know the children but missing Elizabeth. There were no other girls her age and as Anna walked, she thought of all the things she would tell Elizabeth. She looked over at Henry, who was shadowing their father and the other men. He was trying to act like he wasn't tired, but she knew better.

While walking, Anna listened to the noises of the carts and thought of how she and Elizabeth would have laughed, "Every Indian within ten miles would know we are here!" She listened to the sounds of the oxen pulling and straining against their new leather harnesses ... their snorts and grunts ... their hooves clomping along. She heard the creaking of the carts with their wooden wheels clattering on the ground, the slatted sides groaning under their burdens, and the friendly talk of the men in their native German. Anna smiled and wondered who was out there listening ... and watching.

Every now and then, Anna heard stories from home and laughter, but mostly the talk was of more practical matters such as what they might hunt for dinner.

Anna listened closely as a tall man she'd never met insisted, "Corn! Corn will be our first and highest priority when we arrive. We've got to get a field of corn in the ground to harvest before winter. If not, we could all starve."

Another man responded, "After a storehouse, Peter, we can plant corn. We've got to have a place to store our belongings once we arrive. If not, either the rain or the Indians will ruin it all."

Papa asked both men, "Do either of you know how to plant or build?" and by the uncomfortable silence, Anna knew the answer.

She knew the saying, 'Where there is a will, there is a way,' and she hoped it was true, but she also knew 'willing' was just like wishing. It wasn't enough. This might be even more of an adventure than she thought.

Anna looked up to see Henry next to her, nursing a sore finger in his mouth. His face was covered in gray powdery dirt and little tracks of sweat left trails down his face like rivers in a dusty land.

Anna nodded towards Henry, "You've worked hard today with the men. You must be done in. I've hardly seen you at all." Then she teased, "Maybe really you've just been hiding in a wagon and the dust from the wheels made you look like an urchin."

He wiped the sweat from his face and, too tired to even get riled, asked, "So ... have you met very many of the other families yet?"

"A few," Anna sighed. "It's hard to believe they were all in Karlshafen with us at one time or another. Everyone was so scattered in dugout caves along the dunes. We hardly knew anyone else existed. Everyone was just too busy staying alive to be social."

"There are one hundred and twenty people in our group, according to the guides," Henry said, glancing sideways at a beefy man with a very bushy, unkempt beard so long it brushed the front of his shirt. His loud voice and serious, unsmiling expression made Henry nervous and wary around him. He seemed somehow wild and unpredictable.

Finally, they heard the guides call, "Halt" so the animals could rest and everyone could have something to eat. As they all shared a bit of leftover cornbread from breakfast, Henry asked, pointing towards the stranger, "Papa, why does that man want to be here? He's not very friendly, and he doesn't even have a family with him. Will he be staying in Fredericksburg with us, or is he one of the guards who will be returning to New Braunfels?"

His father sighed, "His name is Schmidt, and he has a hard past. He shot a man in Germany – something to do with politics and a duel – and he came to Texas as part of his pardon, to contribute to our protection against the Indians in Fredericksburg. He's experienced with a gun and no-nonsense in his ways. He'll be an asset I hope."

"Can we trust him?" Henry asked, glancing a little nervously toward Schmidt.

Anna broke in, "If he is here with us now, then he wants a second chance. He'll want to stay alive as much as we do, I bet. I'm glad he's here. Sometimes we all need a second chance."

Papa rested a reassuring hand on Anna's shoulder, but warned, "True, liebling*, but we'd be wise to stay watchful and alert."

"And alert for Indians too, right Papa? Are there many different kinds around here?" Anna asked.

"Probably so, Anna, and ja*, there are many." Papa replied. Most of them are Comanche, Lipan Apaches, and Delawares. Delaware, we hope, will be friendly. The Comanche, however, will be our biggest concern. There are thousands of them in the region of Fredericksburg and the land grants, each group with their own chief and their own ideas. Even the Lipan Apaches are afraid of them and have been pushed out of the region mostly.

*Leibling - German for "darling"
*Ja - German for "Yes"

New Braunfels was safely on the edge of Indian Territory, but we are venturing straight into the middle of it. It's not so bad to have men like Schmidt with us when we meet the Comanche," Henry's father admitted honestly.

As they sat talking, two dark-skinned men appeared out of what seemed to be thin air. Under her breath, Anna huffed, "I knew it! I knew we were being watched. How could they miss us? But still, where in the world *did* they come from?"

As they quietly approached, as quietly as if they were walking on clouds, Schmidt with two other men approached them. Without realizing it, the others loosely huddled together near the wagons, tense and worried.

The midday sun beat down on them. All went quiet as if all of Texas was holding its breath. The newcomers were bare-chested other than beaded straps holding a quiver of arrows. They looked at the weary caravan curiously and spoke in a strange combination of their own language and what sounded like some Spanish. Anna and the other Germans understood none of it. The Indians tried and tried to communicate, but finally threw up their hands and gave up, turning to leave.

Letting out their breath, Anna and Henry looked at each other and smiled with relief.

As the group stood watching them go, one of the guards nervously chuckled, "They must be Delaware. That's good, but I sure wish they spoke German!"

Preparing to move forward again, Anna heard the guide say, "The Delaware are immigrants, like us. They used to live all the way up in New York. They were pushed out by the Americans."

Anna thought about this and observed, "You know, Henry, we have a lot in common with the Delaware. They seemed all right. Maybe, like us, they just want a place to live in peace."

Henry was not so sure and warned, "Well, did you see the tomahawk, bow, and arrows they carried? I hope you're right because if they aren't, there's not an awful lot we can do about it." He turned and walked off muttering about not having a gun.

Anna shook her head and hoped he didn't do anything foolish.

4

Wounds

Later, as the sun sank low in the sky, Anna staggered in the tall grass near the edge of the woods collecting sticks for the campfire. She was done in. Next to her, Henry's arms were full. He looked down and said, "There are some, just there. Come on, let's get these and that will be enough. Papa said we need to have the fire going before the sun is down. We need to be settled for the night before it's dark." He awkwardly stooped down, balancing his load, to pick up a large branch.

Henry clumsily uncoiled himself and turned to find where Anna had gone. Without warning, a terrifying scream split the air. A high-pitched scream. Close! Horribly close. It was only a moment, but a hundred things raced through their minds. Was it Indians ... an attack ...?

Anna barely saw the muzzle of a gun before a shot was fired just over her shoulder. Ears ringing and heart thumping, her bundle of sticks clattered to the ground as she threw her arms up and bent her knees – ready.

Her eyes caught the flash of movement before her mind could tell her what she was seeing. A huge cat - it must be a cat, but it was so massive - seemed to float through the air. Its enormous paws and sharp claws reached towards her, its wide mouth open and teeth bared. Anna only managed a small squeak of terror before the brutal beast, larger than a grown man, dropped dead in front of her.

Schmidt, the fierce man Henry was so afraid of, saved them with one dead shot. "Mr. Schmidt," Henry stammered, but Schmidt had already turned and stalked back to camp.

"Tell your young ones to keep alert, Schupp. Panthers live in these parts and like to hunt at dusk. *You'd* be wise to learn to shoot," Schmidt snarled to their father as he passed. "But at least we'll have meat tonight." he growled.

Anna turned to her brother and stammered, with only a small tremor in her voice, "Maybe you *should* learn to shoot." She bent to gather the scattered sticks for the fire, hiding her trembling hands and trying to calm her racing heart.

Papa stood next to them, looking at the limp beast lying on the ground. He said, "Soon, Son, when we arrive. I think it may be time for both of us to learn to shoot. Soon, but not yet. It takes time to learn to handle a firearm well enough for it to be more protection than danger. We will do our part by cleaning and dressing the animal for dinner. It will fill many stomachs tonight."

"But Papa," Henry insisted, "Look around. Every man and boy strong enough to hold one has a gun. Why are we the only ones without one? They all carry them around loaded and cocked in case of attack. What will we do? Hide?" Henry knew he was going a bit too far, but he no longer cared. His face was flushed with heat and frustration and he was shaking all over with the aftershock of near violence.

"Henry," Papa started and then paused, looking heavenward for the right words, "You know that isn't true. There are some others, like me, who were wood-workers or craftsmen of some sort who didn't need a gun in Germany. But, as you see, this is a different time and place. Patience. We will learn soon enough."

After dinner that night, Henry sulked around the camp circle where people gathered to talk about the day. Nervously drumming his fingers on the sides of his legs, he paced, thinking about learning to shoot. He just couldn't let go of the idea.

Henry thought of all the different people in the group. Papa was right in that there were, perhaps, some others that did not have a gun, but they were few. In their group, there were the German settlers, the drivers who drove the oxen pulling the carts, and the guards who guided them safely to Fredericksburg. Everyone except the Germans would be leaving when they arrived. Henry wished they would stay for at least a little while.

One of the drivers who Henry met along the trail, held a beautiful pistol with a silver inlay on the handle. As Henry walked by, he was spit-shining its barrel and holding it out at arm's length to admire it. Henry couldn't resist. Palms sweating, his feet pulled him to the man, and he found himself gazing at the weapon with reverence.

"Can I ... Do you mind ... can I hold it? I'm going to have one someday soon. Papa just said so." Henry breathed with admiration and longing in his voice.

"Sure, lad," he said, grinning and laughing at Henry's awkwardness. "But be careful, that thing is loaded." Putting it into Henry's hands he said, "Go ahead. Get the feel of it. See? Isn't she beautiful?"

All at once there was a flash of heat and a roar from the gun. As if it was on fire, Henry dropped the gun in the dirt and looked around with panic in his eyes. His heart pounded and his face flooded with heat. Then, a sickening feeling in the pit of his stomach began to grow.

Across the gathering, Anna was sobbing in pain. She was curled into a ball gasping and sobbing.

"What have I done? Anna, what have I done?" Frantically Henry made his way through the gathering crowd to where his mother and father were huddled over Anna. Shame and fear washed over him. He was not ready to be a man. He couldn't even handle a gun without shooting someone. No, not just someone ... Anna. In shame, he ran to their cart and beat his fist against the wooden side crying out in anger. How could he have been so stupid?

Then Papa was there, grim-faced and anxious. "Henry," his father said in a stern voice Henry had never heard before, "I've told you holding a gun doesn't make you a man. If you want to be a man, you have to own your responsibilities. Your sister isn't dead, praise God. It's only her foot that is wounded where the bullet grazed her."

Henry raised his face to look at his father. Smears of dirt streaked his cheeks where he'd swiped at his tears. He shuddered as he took a deep breath and said hopefully, "Only her foot? Oh, Papa, that is good."

His father, unable to stay calm blurted, "Yes, Henry, her foot! How is she supposed to walk? How are we supposed to keep it clean? What do we do to keep her from getting a fever or a putrid foot? We've got no medicine, no bandages."

Realizing the fact of this, Henry's shoulders slumped, and he squeezed his eyes shut, trying not to cry.

His father more kindly added, "You have carried a heavy load these past few days, sharing in the work of a man, lifting rocks and building bridges. Now you will have to carry this burden as well; the burden that your sister may yet die from your foolishness. If you indeed want to be a man, you will carry this load with courage and face what may come."

Henry knew the truth of what his father said. He hoped he would be man enough to carry this load. It was a heavier load than he'd ever imagined.

5

Strangers

It was late afternoon on the sixth day of hard travel, and Anna lay sweating in the cart, feeling every bump and jostle of the rough ground under the wheels. She lay propped on some quilts in between the wooden trunks that held their belongings. The precious eggs were cushioned next to her, swaying in their padded crate as if being rocked to sleep. She wished she were as comfortable as those eggs. She grimaced as the cart thudded over a large stone and glanced at Henry to see if he was watching. He was still brooding over the accident for the past three days and walked alongside their family cart for hours. He was keeping a protective eye on her, making sure she did not need to stop for rest or water. They needed to keep up with the group, and no one was in a mind to dawdle on their behalf. Anna felt the open space close around them and press into her heart.

Earlier in the morning, Henry overheard Mama and Papa talking. "William, I'm worried," Mama said. "We've washed Anna's foot with fresh water every day, but it's just not enough. It's beginning to fester and is getting redder and more tender. I know Anna isn't letting on how much it pains her." Then her shoulders slumped and Henry saw her struggle to hold back a sob. "Oh, what will we do? I feel so helpless," she cried.

Papa took Mama by the shoulders and looked her straight in the eye, "Christine, there is nothing we can do but carry on and keep up. If we fall behind, we will be lost and unprotected from attack. All we can do is keep up and pray for a miracle."

As they plodded along over the rocky hills, the wagon creaking noisily, Henry noticed a lone stranger with a beaded leather vest and long drawstring pants approaching their wagon from the rear. Henry muttered to himself and joined Papa in a protective stance between the Indian and their wagon.

Papa soon realized he was asking to trade venison for some of their supply of gunpowder. Because he wore pants and not a breechcloth, they could tell he was from the Delaware group, which were supposed to be one of the friendlier sort of tribes. However, Henry noticed him looking with interest at his sister and her bandaged foot, and he tensed with alarm.

"Papa, no!" Henry whispered fiercely, "We will need that!" but Papa only grimaced at Henry and gave the stranger the precious gunpowder anyway because, as he said, "Small gifts make friends". He hoped they just made a friend.

Picking up pace to catch up with the group, Henry remembered the talk of the men at night around the campfire. They told stories about the savage ways of the Indians, kidnapping young girls and boys to be camp slaves. Sometimes they would adopt them into their tribe and give them Indian names, but other times they treated them harshly and were cruel – beating and starving them. He knew his sister would be an easy target. She certainly could not run to escape an attack. He did not like being in the back of the group and wished for the security of the middle of the pack.

Anna interrupted his brooding, asking, "Henry, how much further will we go today? I'm bored and bruised riding in this cart. I wish I could walk with you. I feel so useless!"

Henry sighed deeply, closed his eyes and let his head droop, his bushy, uncut hair hanging in his eyes.

"Oh Henry, I am sorry," Anna said, brushing a loose strand of hair out of her face. "I didn't mean to say that. My foot will get better soon and then we will laugh about it. It will be one more part of our adventure. Remember, all of life is an adventure, right? We've already had so many, and this will be another that we will talk about when we are old."

Henry smiled a bit and was relieved to see the wagons pull up short to circle around for the night. He said, "Don't worry, Anna. We are stopping now. We'll get camp set early enough to give the men time to find some game to share for dinner and to gather wood for fires. Here, let me help you get down."

He chuckled at the relief in her eyes, but as he looked past her, his laughter died in his throat. "Anna, look, another group of Indians are coming into camp. Stay out of sight. These look different," he warned.

With knitted brows, Anna replied, "They do, don't they? That paint on their cheeks and their spears with skins hanging off of them ... look, Papa and some others are going to talk to them."

Anna poked Henry in the arm and continued, "Go try to listen. Maybe you can find something out."

As everyone began setting up for the night, a murmur ran through the camp, "Lipan Apaches ..."

Then Papa was there, his eyes dark. He said, "Henry, keep your sister comfortable and stay clear of them. Help your mother and keep out of sight. They want to join us around the fire for food and drink. This land, this place is their home. We are strangers to them, and although they don't seem outwardly hostile, they certainly aren't happy to see us. They are, however, happy to eat our food." Papa grunted with a frown.

"Papa", Anna asked as her father bent down to examine her swollen, red foot, "what are those strange hairy things hanging from their spears? They look like nothing I've ever seen."

"Don't worry, Anna," her father said, "stay low and quiet. They will leave soon."

Then, wiping a dirty hand over his face, he turned to Mama and said gravely, "Christine, Schmidt has taken ill. Can you come help? You must come now!" He turned to his son. "Henry, as soon as you get Anna settled, come with your mother to get what she needs for Schmidt."

Henry watched as his father walked back to the group of men making a fire and preparing gifts of food and drink for the Indians. He saw the things Anna asked Papa about. He heard the other men talk of such things at night around the fire, and he knew they weren't any kind of animal. He also knew he didn't want his own blond hair to be the next prized scalp on their belt.

6

Bear Hunt

"I'm fine, really Henry. Go help Mama. She needs you and I will stay put," Anna said, trying to sound better than she felt. "I'm just going to sit here and watch the stars come out. Honestly, I'm never alone on a clear night. The Texas stars are my company." Anna smiled warmly at Henry and gave him a push towards Schmidt's cart, but as soon as he was out of sight, Anna let herself fall onto the quilt and took the deep restoring breaths she needed.

She watched him leave and thought for the hundredth time how much she missed her friend Elizabeth. Was she looking at the night sky and at their lucky star? She imagined the Texas flag, blowing in the wind. In her imagination, God plucked their lucky star from the sky and put it on the flag so they could see it day and night.

Henry approached his mother quietly, so as not to disturb Mr. Schmidt. He saw Schmidt's eyes flutter briefly and close. He was gray. Henry didn't know illness could be a color, but it was. Just yesterday, Schmidt was the color of a ripe peach – yellow blending with pinks and reds – but today he was a ghastly shade of gray. Henry stood frozen and watched his chest rise and fall as if it took all his massive strength to do this small thing.

"Um … Mama." Henry started to say uncomfortably, "What can I do? Is there any help I can give?"

Hearing Henry's voice, Schmidt opened his eyes and tried to focus. "Come here," he said weakly, stretching his hand towards him. Henry stepped closer and, wiping his sweating palms on his dusty pants, squatted near him and looked straight into Schmidt's eyes. His face may have been gray, but his eyes were on fire. There was still something to say, and Henry was going to listen.

"When I was young, I went hunting for bear," Schmidt began, talking through the pain, struggling for breath. "I was ill-prepared and foolish … to hunt bear," he said haltingly. "You have to know how to track … and to think like a bear."

Henry looked at him, puzzled over this strange story and wondered if it might be the fever making him confused. After a quick glance at Mama, he replied, his voice cracking, "Yes sir, I'm listening."

Schmidt went on, laboring for air. "Bears will rage against you if ... you ... are not smart. They can be dangerous and fierce ... fierce predators."

Having heard of the savage brown bears in the German Forests, Henry knew a little of what Schmidt seemed to be thinking. He knew that in America, there were bears called grizzlies that were like their brown bear. The native brown bear in Germany was smart, protective, and fought to the death. When he was a boy, he remembered seeing a man visiting their town with deep, terrible scars that began on his face and ran all the way down one arm. Everyone whispered, "He surprised a bear while hunting, and it almost cost him his life."

Schmidt collapsed in exhaustion and Henry, thinking he was asleep, started to rise. Then he heard Schmidt say quietly while waving his hand slowly about, "This was to be my final bear hunt. This time I was ready." And very quietly, so low that Henry wasn't sure he heard him, said, "You will learn to hunt bear in this place. You will learn to be a man."

Schmidt said no more but fell into an exhausted sleep. "It is his heart," his mother said sadly. "Perhaps it is just not strong enough to carry him where he wants to go."

While Henry gathered some wood for Mama, he considered this, and murmured quietly to himself, "And his final bear hunt may come too late."

Skirting quietly around the Indians, Henry returned to Anna to check on her and to take her some food. It was good food; a stew of deer meat and wild onions that made Henry's mouth water. Around the campfire, he noticed those new fierce Indians eyeing Schmidt from a distance, gesturing to one another and rubbing their own whiskerless chins. Schmidt did have an impressive beard. One any man might admire for its fullness and length. Henry hoped one day to have a beard like that.

Anna pushed the food around on her plate and mumbled, "I'm not hungry, Henry. You can have mine." Seeing the look on his face, she said, "But don't worry, I don't need much food to just sit all day. You need more to be able to walk and do all the chores."

She carefully propped her foot up on the side of a trunk, which helped with the pulsing throb that seemed to echo her heartbeat. Henry's stomach was always eager for more food. He glanced at Anna's leftover food and started to reach for it. But then, he glanced at her foot and all thoughts of hunger were gone. He only wondered again at the color of illness. Schmidt was gray, but Anna's foot was scarlet red.

"Oh Anna," Henry said, alarmed, "I need to get some water to rinse your foot. It looks bad." As he rose and turned to pick up the bucket, he kicked the side of the cart in frustration at his own foolishness in wanting to hold the gun. He knew the saying well from his opa*, "all that glitters is not gold." In disgust at his own stupidity, he was learning a hard lesson. Would it cost him his sister?

Infection and illness were two things they were powerless to fight in this wild place. He knew why they wanted to leave Germany; to find opportunity and to escape power-hungry men who used politics as their weapons. Would this place allow them

Opa - German for "Grandfather"

to make a new start? Would this place ever seem like home? Would they survive long enough to find out? Henry thought he understood what Schmidt was saying. This new place with its fierce challenges was to be their bear and he would have to learn to hunt, to be smarter than the bear.

7

The Grave

In the morning, Anna knew something was off. The camp was busy but oddly quiet. "Schmidt is gone," Mama said simply with tears in her eyes. "His heart gave out during the night." She didn't say more. Anna felt there was nothing to say. It was another death, another tragedy along this never-ending trail across Texas.

As the day began, everyone mourned the ill-tempered man they barely knew.

They mourned the loss of the sheer force of his will and the strength of his desire to move forward every day. Anna silently wondered if they would make it without him.

The day seemed to sense their mood, and was gray with low clouds, threatening to leave them with broken wagon wheels and soggy feet.

To Henry, Schmidt was a man to be respected. Henry knew there were some troubles in Schmidt's past. The man was foolish once, but so was Henry. Schmidt was not an evil person. In Germany, he was caught in the middle of an impossible situation. His father was right, Schmidt learned from his mistakes and had deserved a second chance. Difficulties in life, he saw now, were a bear – one with fierce claws and teeth, willing to attack and fight to the death.

Schmidt's bear hunt was over, but Henry's was only beginning. He would miss Schmidt and his gruff manner and bushy beard.

"Henry," his father said, jerking him out of his thoughts. "Schmidt is gone, and we must carry his memory with us. We will have a burial service this morning, then we must move on quickly to make our day's journey before nightfall."

His father continued, putting a big hand on Henry's shoulder, "As you know, Schmidt's rifle was a good one, the one he used to shoot the panther, and I have been able to purchase it at a good price from The Society. When we get to Fredericksburg, we will learn to shoot properly, and we will honor Schmidt when we do. After all, he is the one who said you needed to learn to shoot," Henry's father said with a sad smile.

Henry took a deep breath. Then he and his father, with some other men, struggled in the rocky soil to dig a grave for Schmidt, stacking some large rocks as a headstone. As they worked, Henry was certain they were being watched. He was sure he caught glimpses of movement in the trees nearby. He wondered if the Indians were always watching them, always one step ahead of them.

After they were on their way, having said some words on Schmidt's behalf in the company of the entire group, they walked in silence beside the cart. Anna rode again, in the cart, sneaking fretful glances at her foot and at Henry. She told herself, "This *will* be an adventure I'll be able to tell my grandchildren one day. I *will not* die like Schmidt." She tried with all her might to not ask herself the terrible question, *"Would* I?"

Mama interrupted the silence with a gasp of alarm. In the chaos of the morning, she left behind her only cooking pot, the heavy cast-iron skillet, next to the fire, where she was boiling water to sterilize bandages for Anna's

foot. Every single household necessity was just that ... a necessity. Without it, they would not cook. There were no shops here, no way to make a new one. They must go back.

"I will go," Henry said. "We are only twenty minutes from the campsite. I am fast and can run it in fifteen minutes."

Henry's father hesitated but agreed. With Anna's foot, they could not be separated from the group. Their only choice was to keep moving.

Swiftly, Henry returned down the same trail. The ground was soft with spring grass, and he ran quietly, taking the shortest route through the tree growth whenever possible. Part of his attention was on the ground and the other part on the fact there always seemed to be Indians about. They seemed to be everywhere and nowhere at the same time. He felt invisible eyes on him and The Society at every moment. Were they friends or enemies? He was not sure at all, but the Indians would decide one way or the other. As for him, he'd be happy to get along and be friends so long as once they reached their destination in the hills of Texas, and they could make a home.

He missed his home in Germany and the sausages with sauerkraut* his Mama and Oma used to make. Henry remembered the house his father built. That was before. That was when Germany was a place they wanted to call home.

*Sauerkraut – Cabbage which has been cut into strips and pickled.

His father once designed and worked on several houses in their town, carving intricate woodwork figures around the windows and on the mantle. William Schupp was once an important man in their community.

As Henry rounded the last corner, breathing heavily from his effort, he spied the smothered remains of the fire and Mama's wayward pot. He reached down to pick it up, and as he turned, he froze in his tracks. There, just below him, at the bottom of the small rise, were the Apache Indians who were at his camp last night; the ones with the savage ornaments of hair and scalp hanging from their belts. They were standing over the open grave and adding another ornament to their belt.

Not able to help himself, he cried out, the sound escaping from his throat before he knew what happened. At once they looked right at him, their eyes boring into him. But he could not turn away or leave his friend with an open grave.

"No!" Henry shouted. "No, you can't do this. It is wrong!" but Henry knew his words in German meant nothing to them.

With a warning in their eyes, and waving their tomahawks, they shouted and whooped. They said, "Amigo, Vamos a qui!*" moving steadily but slowly towards him.

With each step they took towards Henry, he took one back from them, slowly backing away. But he could not let it go.

* *Spanish for "Friend, come here!"*

"Please! Please close the grave," he said, talking with his hands as well as with his words. With each slow step away, he pleaded.

Then, before they could change their minds, and add his scalp to their collection, Henry turned and fled, still clutching Mama's ash-stained iron skillet in one hand and saying one last goodbye to Schmidt in his heart.

8

Friend or Foe

Tears of fury were burning Henry's eyes by the time he caught up to the steadily plodding caravan of carts. The pot landed with a loud clank as Henry thrust it in the back of the cart.

"What is it, Henry?" Anna blurted, "What?"

"Nothing!" Henry shouted as he stormed past and launched into a deep conversation with Papa that included a lot of gesturing, waving of arms, and tears.

Anna wasn't stupid and she wasn't a coward. She was not fragile, like the eggs in the cart next to her. She would know in due time, but she would let Henry vent first. "It is better to let him vent to someone else," she muttered. Besides, her foot hurt too much for her to bother with Henry just now. It pounded with every bump of the heavy cart as it jostled over rocks, tufts of prairie grass and ruts in the ground.

"Mama, will we stop soon to rest the animals and eat?" Anna asked, through clenched teeth as her mother approached. Anna could read her mother like a book. She saw the deep lines between her brows and knew she was worried.

Mama sighed, shaking her head and leaning over to touch Anna's arm. "You look feverish, child. Yes, before too long, I think we will have a short break.

But we must still travel a while today." Mama picked up the wayward pot and tried to brush off the ash, but it clung to it like the gray sky clung to the treetops.

"Mama," Anna said with a question in her voice, "there sure seems to be a lot of Indians. More than I ever imagined. Do you think they mind us being here?"

"Anna, you are a brave and adventurous girl. You should know the truth of it or as much of it as we can even understand." Mama said with tired eyes. "There are many different Indian tribes in the Texas hills. With the new War with Mexico, there is very little protection for settlers like us. Almost all of the fighting men of Texas are there, struggling to keep Texas free from Mexico. And here we are – left to fight our own battles. But we have John Meusebach, on our side. He is the

Commissioner-General of The Society, and is a wise man. He will make treaties with the Indians for us. We must trust him."

Mama stumbled slightly on the rough terrain, as she walked beside the cart, and reached out a hand to brace herself.

Anna, tired as she was, wanted to reassure Mama, and said, "When the treaties are made, the Indians will keep their side of the bargain. I think they are watching us all the time, and they can see we don't want war. I think it will be all right, Mama."

Mama replied, "I hope so, Anna, but we cannot stray from the group. With so many eyes on us, we are in danger alone."

Leaning back on the quilt and gazing at the gray sky, Anna tried to think of their new homestead.

"Hmmm... do you think we will arrive in Fredericksburg in time to plant a garden and to have fresh beans and cabbage for the summer?" Anna wondered aloud.

Mama laughed a little sadly and said, "We'll start with corn. Lots of corn. We will have to wait for wheat once the parts for a mill are found. What good is wheat without a mill? But we will plant a small garden by the house as soon as we can." Then she sighed, "I can't wait to have a roof over our heads and a kitchen. Oh, to have fresh bread, schnitzel*, and beer!"

Anna groaned, not in pain, but in memory, "Oh Mama, I do miss the schnitzel, but what I really miss is the gingerbread!

*Schnitzel – meat, thinned by pounding and coated with egg and bread crumbs and fried.

The kind you made was my favorite, especially when we could decorate them for Christmas! And in our new town, we will have a school, right? I've missed so much school!"

"Oh Anna, you know we will have school. We Germans are proud of our education. School AND societies ..."

Her mother laughed, in spite of herself, "Oh there will be plenty of societies! You know – singing societies, and then shooting societies ... dancing societies. You can be sure we will have them all. Those will come in due time, but first will be a church and a school."

Finally, they stopped to rest and eat. As Mama handed out the stale bread, she said, "This is the last of it. From now on, the men will have to find wild game to keep us full."

Anna added, "Oooh, maybe we will find more wild peaches along the trail too."

Henry's mouth watered as he remembered the juicy, ripe fruit with the fuzzy skin. His stomach growled as he imagined eating wild game roasted over a fire and the sweet fruit. He was tired of the tough dried meat and stale bread they ate along the trail.

"Henry," Mama said, shaking him back to the present, "help me move Anna so I can change her bandage and wash her foot."

As they were pulling the quilt straight, a single Indian appeared at the top of the hill and made his way directly towards their wagon. Henry tensed, bracing himself for anything. With fury in his eyes, he walked towards him and shouted, "What? What do you want? Leave us alone. We don't need you or want you here!"

Anna was shocked and said, "Henry! He means us no harm. He is a Delaware, you can see, and alone. Let's see what he wants. It's a good thing he can't speak German! You are being horrible to him!"

Anna felt sure the Indian meant them no harm, but Papa, returning from loosening and cobbling the oxen that pulled their cart, put himself between the Indian and his family. Unlike Henry, however, he welcomed him into their camp, offering him some of their precious dried meat.

Henry sulked, but allowed the Indian to approach without further protest. Delaware or not, he did not trust him.

The man was short, but broad-shouldered and strong. He wore a large, loose-fitting sleeveless shirt with a leather strap at his waist and leather leggings. Brightly colored beads hung from the fringe of his shirt and were woven in around his neck. Over his shoulder, he carried a drinking horn, bow and quiver, as well as a small round pouch decorated with fringe with red and yellow beads in the shape of a star. He was proud, but Anna could tell he was kind.

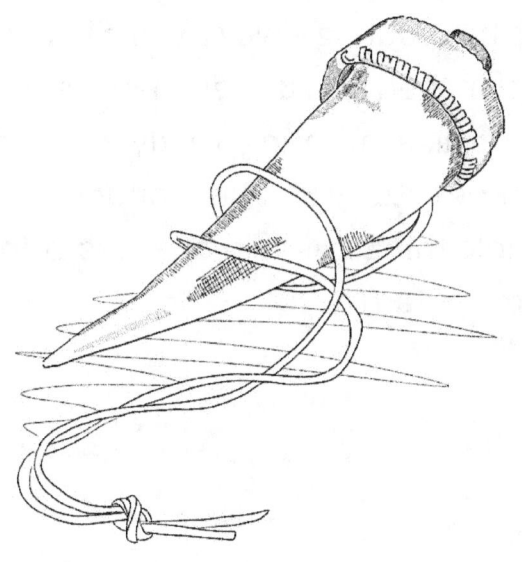

"Hey, I recognize him. He's the one we saw yesterday, who came wanting to trade venison for gunpowder," Henry exclaimed. He remembered how he looked at his sister's foot and wondered again if he was targeting them as a weak link, one that could easily be captured and taken as a slave for their tribe.

Was he here to find out more? Was he scouting a way to take his sister? He clenched and unclenched his hands, coiling like a spring ready for action. With deep distrust, he wondered what terrible thing this wild one was going to do to his family.

9

A Gift

The Indian standing in front of their wagon seemed to Anna to be serious but kind with deep crevices between his eyes and on his steep brow. His black hair was pulled back tightly, woven into two thin braids and wrapped around with a piece of leather. There was a single feather hanging from each braid, and Anna watched in a daze of pain as they blew and twisted in the breeze. Around and around they went as if they too were without protection or hope.

While his father was unpacking a crate to find the dried meat to share, Henry picked up the only weapon he could find, his mother's heavy cast-iron skillet that hung from a hook on the back of the wagon. He waved it at the Indian, holding it in both hands, and said, "I'm warning you ... stay away from my sister!"

The Indian raised both hands and slowly reached for the knife at his belt. He waved it at Henry, as if to say, "Step aside, I can hurt you but don't want to." It was a large, worn looking blade with dark stains of blood on the handle. Anna hoped it was usually used for hunting and not fighting.

It was then that Anna looked into his eyes for the first time. They were a beautiful brown, the color of gingerbread. Anna shouted, "Henry, stop it right now. Let him come." And then added a little softer but just as intently, "He has *not* come to do evil. I see it in his eyes."

Henry gradually realized, through his fog of outrage from his earlier encounter, the Indian was gesturing with signs towards his sister. With quick hands, he was indicating he wanted to see Anna's wound and patted the pouch at his waist. Mama, unwrapping it to put on fresh bandages, finished the unwrapping and stepped back, inviting him to look. It was a dangerous, angry looking wound, and Anna winced at the sight of it.

With a careful eye, the visitor gazed at Anna's foot, gently probing it. Then he withdrew a strange smelling powder from his pouch and began to apply it to the wound. It was bitter smelling and stung. Anna winced in pain but trusted those gingerbread eyes.

The Indian finished and gave a kind smile to Anna, a stern look to Henry, and a gesture of friendship to Mama and Papa. Then he turned his back and casually walked away without another backward glance.

Anna, wide-eyed with wonder, said, "I will be better now. I know I will. I can feel it in my heart."

"Anna," Mama confessed, "I never imagined Indians would show kindness to us or care if we lived or died. How narrow-minded I feel."

Henry, less convinced, said, "Well, what choice is there at this point? Anna's foot is only getting worse." He lifted one shoulder in a lopsided shrug and shook his sweaty head slowly back and forth as if to drop the pieces of a confusing puzzle into place.

Anna said, "But, Henry, we need to take kindness when it is given and give it in return when we can. I guess they aren't all that different from us if you think of the good things and terrible things that people did in our own country."

Henry silently agreed and wondered, "Why do you suppose people do such terrible, terrible things?

As they set camp that night, the large clouds rolling in matched Henry's mood. He was filled with such mixed emotions; he could hardly sort them out. The clouds – some puffed up with the promise of a nice day and others dark with threat – mirrored his confusion.

As Papa laid some freshly gathered wood next to the fire, he said, "Henry, you know I am proud of you. It's terribly hard to see the good in people once you've seen the evil we are capable of. You've learned the hard lesson that evil is a path that some men take, but it is their choice. Your choice is to do good and show kindness. I hope it will always be your choice. No one can take that away from you."

With a shrug of his shoulders, Henry tried to smile at his father, but glancing at Anna, he mumbled, "She's the strong one, never complaining, just enduring pain caused by others. Do you think the Indian's medicine will help?"

Papa smiled a little, and said, "I sure hope so, Henry. I hope so."

The next few days were thankfully uneventful. They were filled with the usual breakfasts of fried corn muffins and bacon from wild hogs cooked in the cast iron skillet, packing and loading the wagon, and endless miles of walking.

At the end of each day, their reward was usually fresh game cooked over the open fire. And each day the

Indian with the gingerbread eyes, whose name turned out to be Running Deer, returned. He continued to apply herbs he kept in the beautiful beaded pouch to Anna's foot, mixing them in the palm of his hand with a small amount of water, creating a paste that would dry and crust over her wound. He would talk in his strange tongue as if speaking to the wound itself. And each day, Anna's wound was a little better.

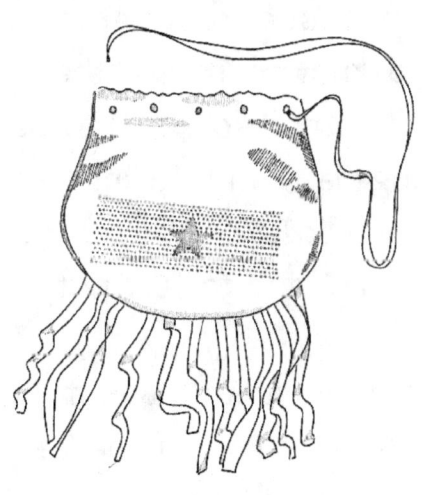

"Henry," Anna wondered one morning, "where do you think Running Deer's village is? How far do you think he comes to see me every day? Just think, somewhere nearby, there is a whole village of Indians, with families like ours."

Henry laughed, "Anna, with as many words of his language you are learning, you will be our translator and go into business as a medicine woman! You certainly are making a name for yourself with our group. At least we've gotten to know some of the families better. It seemed so weird to be going to a strange land with strangers."

Anna replied, "Yes, it is nice to have friends again, and to feel not quite so alone."

On the eighth day of Running Deer's visit, as they watched an eagle soar overhead with wings spread wide,

Anna announced, "Henry! I feel so much better. I feel as if I could soar with that eagle! Running Deer calls it an òpalanie. He is a beautiful creature! What do you suppose he sees up there? Do you think he sees our new home?"

With a short laugh, Henry replied, "Anna, I wish we could soar like the eagle, then we could fly the rest of the way! I am so tired of walking!"

In a playful mood once more, Anna grinned as she replied, "Well, then, let's just ask him to give us a ride! He seems big enough to carry you off. You are so skinny!"

Henry was relieved to have his sister back. He pretended to be offended, and said, "Well, if I was riding the whole time, perhaps I wouldn't be so skinny! I'm still doing all your chores, remember?"

Anna replied, "Tomorrow I will walk," and she meant it.

10

The Village

The next day began with a slight chill in the air. As Anna stretched, she plucked a dreadfully uncomfortable rock from under her blanket and tossed it down the low rise near their camping spot. It would be another long day of travel, but nothing could dampen her excitement of this being her first day to walk again.

"Up, Henry, wake up!" Anna cried, "What a beautiful bright blue sky and just listen to the birds! They are telling you to get up and get going!"

Henry mumbled and rolled over, saying, "No they aren't. They are telling you to leave me alone and to go back to sleep ..."

"Oh, do get up Henry, today I will walk again!" Anna replied as she picked up the edge of the quilt they were sleeping on and yanked, toppling Henry off and rolling him onto the rocky ground.

"Ouch! Ok, ok ... I'm up. Boy, you were nicer when you were hurt. Maybe the cart will roll over your foot and you will have to ride again." Henry gruffed, brushing the leaves out of his hair.

Anna just smirked and began to shake out the quilt to pack for the day. Their camping spot, in a small clearing under the canopy of beautiful oak trees with giant twisting branches, reminded them both of the dark forests in Grimm's Fairy Tales.

Last night, Anna entertained her brother and the few other camp children with the tale of Hansel and Gretel. A tall gangly boy named John about Henry's age was there, laughing at her stories and encouraging Henry to do mischief. Anna could tell he and Henry were going to be friends. She would need to watch her back around those two.

Thinking now of the Grimm tales, she loved the bravery of the children who faced the evil witch that lived in the forest. Those fairy tale children used their wits to free themselves from her grasp. In the dark of the night, with the cry of wolves in her ears and the firelight casting shadows in the branches of the trees, Anna could well imagine the fear of Hansel and Gretel. Even though she knew they were just made-up stories, their courage helped strengthen her when she was scared. She loved almost all the Grimm tales, especially Cinderella, Rumpelstiltskin, Little Red Riding Hood, and of course, Hansel and Gretel.

Perhaps she would tell the story of Rumpelstiltskin tonight and imagine being locked in the castle spinning gold from straw. Too bad they could not really spin straw into gold. It would be rough going for a while after they finally made it to Fredericksburg and settled in. She overheard enough talk between Mama and Papa about their plans to know that they would be dependent on The Society for food and supplies for the first year, until there was enough time to grow crops, plant a garden, and harvest their own corn.

Anna commented to Henry, while they were packing their things back into the wagon, "You know we're putting up a town in the absolute middle of nowhere. There won't be any trade routes or waterways. Nothing and no one. It will be us and the wilderness." She shrugged her shoulders and added, "If we don't harvest a crop, we could starve ... I overheard a lot of things while riding in the cart. People seemed to forget I was there."

"I overheard the same things when John and I were quietly walking near the men. Everyone's getting worried the further we get from civilization. Maybe the Delaware Indians will be willing to trade with us," Henry speculated while gesturing with his chin toward an approaching Indian. There seemed to be more of them farther from New Braunfels.

At noon, Running Deer came to visit and walked alongside their cart silently as if he were waiting for something. By mid-afternoon, Anna was riding in the cart again, not wanting to aggravate her foot too much. Anna was glad she was able to walk again, for at least part of the day, and she gave Running Deer a grateful smile. She liked walking more than a bruised backside and stiff muscles from the jostling cart. Today, the sun was warm and insects buzzed around them as they rounded the hills, circling their bases to avoid strain on the oxen.

As they rounded a large hill with scrub trees clinging to its side and began a downhill descent into the Pedernales River basin, Anna's eyes went wide with astonishment. "Look!" she cried. "An Indian village! Oh, it's huge ... and wonderful!"

Running Deer laughed at the look on Anna's face and turned, walking toward a family of Indians in the distance. They were clustered along the banks of the river, busy hanging fish on a rack to dry.

As they came fully into view, a whoop went up from the camp and three Indians on horseback galloped quickly to the front of the convoy.

"Oh! They were expecting us!" Anna blurted.

"Yes," Papa cautioned. "There are many of them and few of us ... I hope our guides know what they are doing, crossing the river here."

"Oh Papa, it will be alright. Running Deer has always been kind. Look, at their houses! They are just sticks and skins. And look at the racks of fish! And the children!"

Papa laughed, "Hold on there, Anna. You are going to fall off the cart if you aren't careful. Settle down now!" Then growing serious, he added, "We need to keep our wits about us. They seem friendly, but we really don't know, do we?"

Anna continued to stare at the horses tied to stakes and hundreds of women and children busy at their chores. Some women sewed clothing made of leather; others were weaving baskets or cooking food. The children were carrying water, watching younger toddlers, or playing. In a pen on the far side of camp, there were horses with feathers in their flowing manes. They were beautiful and fierce-looking.

Delaware Indians of all ages stopped what they were doing and watched, staring openly. Their eyes showed a mixture of distrust, curiosity, and defiance.

Mama, with a worried look on her face, drew near the cart. Anna could see her knuckles turning white from squeezing her fists and trying to stay calm. Gently placing a protective hand on her arm, Papa replied with more confidence than he felt, "This is the only low water crossing for miles. They know this, and our guide was sure it would be okay."

Many prayers and nervous voices were heard for the next hour, as they lumbered with their heavily loaded carts to the edge of the Pedernales River and then painstakingly across it.

Anna knew Mama was scared. A shiver ran down her own spine as she watched all the Indians watching them, but she would not show her fear; she just would not. She sat tall in the wagon, holding the crate of eggs in her lap so they would not spill out while crossing the river.

Papa explained, "The scouts are crossing the river now, to find the best route. We will wait here and prepare to cross." Suddenly, Anna heard the crack of a gun and cries from the far bank. Henry yelped and Anna stifled a scream as they heard shouts of "Attack!" and mass confusion broke out among the wagons. In a flash, Papa was at their side, saying, "Henry, if we're under attack, we're trapped. If the attacking Indians are on the other side of the river, and we are on this side next to the village, we must all be very brave."

Caught in the panic, Anna cried out, "Mama! Our beautiful eggs! I knew we should have eaten them for dinner!"

And then it was over. The word was passed joyfully along the caravan,

"No attack! No attack! It was a bear! Bring a big knife! We will have bear for dinner!"

"And we still have our eggs!" Henry laughed as the tension left them all and tears of relief spilled down their cheeks.

With a grin, Henry leaned over and patted Anna's hand, saying, "Little sister, we thought we were under attack, and your concern was for eggs more than your scalp!" But he admitted, "Well, those are beautiful eggs ...."

Laughing, Anna swatted her brother's hand and replied, "Perhaps I like eggs more than I like *your* scalp! We all have our priorities!"

As the first wagons forded the river, Running Deer approached their cart with a small girl on his shoulders. She was maybe five or six years old and held something small in her hands. It was a corn husk doll like the ones she saw in Karlshafen so many months ago. The girl handed it to Anna with a smile, and Anna, smiling in return, responded, "Danke, danke schön*. What a lovely doll!"

As the last carts crossed the river and they continued on their way, Anna and Henry waved goodbye to Running Deer and his daughter.

*Danke schön – German for "thank you very much".

"Maybe Running Deer was thinking of his own young daughter when he helped me." Anna thought, watching the village fade. "Other settlers may call these wild ones uncivilized, but I know civility is more than manners. If kindness and mercy are a part of civility, then these wild ones are quite civil indeed," Anna declared, waving one last time towards the village.

11

Fredericksburg

After crossing the river, everyone seemed to have a renewed impatience to get to where they were going. They were just flat beat and their nerves were raw from the encounter with the Delaware village.

Henry, running back to the wagon, panted, "It won't be long now! If we press hard through the afternoon, we can arrive by nightfall. Can you imagine! After so long, we will be there!"

Anna clambered out of the wagon, replying, "I'm going to walk! I want to walk into our new hometown! Isn't it beautiful here?" As she walked, she stooped and picked a handful of wildflowers with yellow and red blooms. She handed one to Henry, and teased, "Put it in your buttonhole. You want to be well dressed when you come home after being gone your whole life."

Henry smirked, and tossed the flower back to her, saying "I'm no dandy! My new home will love me how I am. I am a rough, tough Texan!"

"We are tough, Henry. We've sailed across the ocean, survived the rain and sickness in Karlshafen, and walked all the way across Texas! I guess I'm a tough Texan too." Anna replied, standing up tall and straight.

"Papa," Henry asked, "where will we live when we get there?"

"Well," Papa replied, "first we will all make one common structure – a large storeroom – for everyone to keep their most important things, like food supplies and ammunition, until we can each build our own house. I'll be very

busy helping with the construction, and you'll help alongside me. We will also have to do our share of work in the field. Together all of the families are going to plow and plant a cornfield, to make sure we all have a harvest the first year. Anna and Mama will be busy helping with the work as well. If you thought you were tired before, just you wait. You will have plenty of muscles when we are done."

Overhearing the conversation, Anna chimed in, "But when will we know where we will build our house?"

Papa shrugged his shoulders and said, "The Society will distribute the plots. The money we invested back in Germany has paid for that as well as other things. Soon we will have a proper house."

As the sun grew lower in the sky, their friend John walked over to their wagon and said, "They're going to make a bonfire tonight, and we'll pitch tents tight around it, for protection. Let's see if we can get ours close together. There will be a big feast with the bear meat and much celebrating. Oh, what fun we'll have tonight! Anna, you have to tell us another story!"

On and on they walked, through a dense forest of trees, so thick they could hardly see their way. Then, as if coming out of a dream, they were there, in front of a broken down, partially built log structure of some kind.

Papa said, "That is the storehouse started by the scouts The Society sent to stake out Fredericksburg's location. It looks like they didn't last too long...."

"But we are here now. We will give it the care it needs," Anna said quietly, as everyone entered the clearing in an awed hush. It was a quiet and lonely place, but it would soon be their home and filled with the noise of life.

Then Anna's voice joined the rest in shouts and whoops. Mama's tears of joy showed in her eyes as she said, "No resting now. Not yet. We can celebrate properly tonight, but we must push to set up camp while there is still a little light. It is May 8th, and sixteen days ago we left New Braunfels. Well done, children!"

As she worked next to Mama, Anna sighed and said, "This will be a day we will never forget! It's beautiful! So many trees! Papa will have plenty of wood to build strong houses! Look, the trees stretch to the sky!" She continued as she looked around in amazement at the forest, the creek, and the long arms of the trees, reaching out in every direction. "The flowers!" she said in amazement. "What a beautiful carpet God has given us."

John walked over to Anna and said, "Anna, tonight it will need to be Little Red Riding Hood! Everyone will want to hear that one!" And with mischief in his eyes, he continued, "Can't you see the eyes in the forest looking at us? I think a wolf is there looking at us now! Where is that red cape of yours? You didn't leave it in Germany, I hope."

Then suddenly Anna heard soft growls coming from behind a large oak with low, twisting limbs not five feet away. Its long shadows from the setting sun surrounded her. Could it really be a wolf? She gasped and fear washed over her as Henry leapt out from behind the tree and started whooping with laughter.

"Oh, you two!" she exclaimed, "Stop that! No one will sleep a wink tonight because of you! But ...," she continued with a glint in her own eyes and catching her breath, "Perhaps I will change the story so the wolf tricks some boys named Henry and John, and he will gobble *them* up! Come on, help me with this crate and you can tease me later."

They crossed the clearing and saw Papa stop and wipe his face with a rag. Stopping near him and putting down the crate, Anna looked around curiously at the short stumps of trees in the small clearing around the skeleton of the abandoned building.

Papa read her thoughts and said, "The scouts from The Society started it, but they ran out of food and supplies, so they just left it. They left, but they buried some tools nearby for us to use if we can find them."

"Ran out of food and supplies?" Anna repeated, questioningly. "Left? I promise I will never do that! I can't imagine ever going back."

Papa laughed when he saw her determined look. "I have no doubt in your promise, but don't worry, we've invested a small fortune in The Society, and in exchange they'll supply us with what we need. Now that we are here, we can finish the storehouse, plow fields, and build some houses. The Society will send regular wagon loads of goods from New Braunfels and will keep it all safely stored for us in the headquarters we will build. We'll be able to withdraw food and supplies as we need them, so long as our investment lasts."

Smiling widely, Anna said, "Just watch, Papa. We'll be happy here! We're going to celebrate tonight! Henry said we're making a bonfire and will feast on bear!"

As she walked back toward their cart, weighed down with its heavy load, Anna thought about their journey. They were here at last! In some ways leaving

Germany seemed so long ago. Hard memories of the journey flooded back to her. Now they would have time to make friends, work in the garden, and one day, cook in their new home. Maybe they would even be able to make gingerbread cookies again. They came this far, so she knew they could do anything.

Part 2

August, 1846
Fredericksburg, Texas

"How can we know who we are and where we are going if we don't know anything about where we have come from and what we have been through, the courage shown, the costs paid, to be where we are?" ~ **David McCullough**

12

Captured

It was a hot day in August as Anna and her friend, Elizabeth, walked towards Anna's house. "Let's hurry, Elizabeth. We'll get the lunchpails and sneak up on John and Henry."

"Ja," Elizabeth added as she hurried her pace to match Anna's, "let's sneak through the trees behind old man Adam's house. That way we can get a good view and watch for just the right moment to jump out and scare them."

As they approached the one room fachwerk* house, Mama called, "Have you finished your chores? No running off until they are done. You know I need your help until after the corn is harvested. Until then your father and Henry have to work the fields, and you have to pull extra weight."

Fachwerk - also known as half-timbering, is a traditional timber framing method used to build houses.

"Yes, Ma'am," Anna replied, glancing at her friend. This reminder came every day. Anna didn't fault Mama though. They were all working hard and would continue to work hard if they wanted to make it through the year without starving.

The best part was, though, after Elizabeth arrived a month earlier, they began helping each other with their morning chores – gathering eggs, sweeping the house, and bringing water from the well.

"Do you remember the day your wagon rolled into Fredericksburg?" Anna asked Elizabeth.

Smiling, Elizabeth replied, "You were so excited to see me, you ran all the way down the street and were nearly trampled by a horse!"

"Yes, but you almost broke your neck jumping from the wagon before it stopped!" Anna laughed in reply. "Well, it was a wonderful day, and now I have someone who will share chores with me."

"And someone to listen to your stories." Elizabeth added. "I like the ones about the wild forests and caves like the ones we saw near New Braunfels. And about the Indians too. Especially ones that include Running Deer and Jim Shaw."

Anna liked to include her two favorite Indians as the heroes of her stories. She told Elizabeth about how Running Deer saved her life, about Jim Shaw, the chief of Running Deer's tribe, and the Delaware camp on the Pedernales River. Jim often acted as a go-between for them with the Comanche and as a guide in unfamiliar territories. The Delaware were always welcome in Fredericksburg, and Anna looked forward to their visits.

"Girls!" Mama snapped, "Did you hear me? You two chatter on so, you don't even know what is going on in front of your nose."

"I'm sorry Mama," Anna replied, noticing with guilt how tired Mama looked.

"Go inside and get the lunchpails. There is one for the two of you to share and one for John and Henry. Please be careful with them. No more spilling them while playing tag or leaping about on rocks," Mama continued, looking Anna in the eye and shaking an accusing finger at her.

"Yes, Mama," Anna replied. "We'll take care. Don't worry. And when I get back, I'll help you in the garden. We won't be long."

Anna and Elizabeth took the pails and started towards the river to the place John and Henry liked to rest at lunch and put their feet in the cool water. However, as soon as they rounded the corner, they changed course and headed towards Mr. Adam's house and the cool quiet of the trees behind it, down river from where the boys lounged. They grinned at each other as they secretly plotted their surprise.

Henry and John sat on a rocky ledge overlooking Town Creek, dangling their toes in the water. After working in the large communal corn field all morning long, harvesting some of the early corn alongside the other boys and men, the boys were hot and covered in grime. Most of the men, including their fathers, went home to rest and have lunch at noon. Henry and John, though, liked to come to the river to tell stories of home, joke with one another and cool off.

Henry looked at John and laughed, "My Mama says we are always getting in sticky situations, but we aren't! Well, if you don't count the time with the beehive and honey...."

John, thinking of the sweet, gooey honey, replied, "It was worth every sting! But what about the time you dressed up Mr. Meuller's billy goat in that jacket and strapped a hat to its head? All the other goats ran in terror!"

"Well, it was your fault too, since it was your idea! It took us days to gather them all back. We had to go all the way to Bear Creek to find them all!" Henry chuckled.

"Oh well," John sighed as he enjoyed the peace of the cool river, "what are friends for but to get you into trouble?"

With a mischievous twinkle in his eye, Henry suggested, "Hey John, I know what. Let's find some rocks that are the same size as the corn. We can put them in Herr Mueller's bag while he is gone!

He is such a stinkstiefel*, always telling everyone else to work harder, while he takes breaks all the time. That is unless you are a hosenscheißer* and are afraid to get into trouble."

With a grin, John jumped up and exclaimed, "I am no hosenscheißer! I'll find the best rocks. You just sit here and dangle your girly toes in the cool water and watch me!" he continued as he turned, rolling up his pants and wading across a shallow spot to where some better rocks were on the other side.

John wandered along the bank, looking intently into the shallows for some smooth rocks, while Henry lay on his side, grinning at his friend doing all the work.

* stinkstiefel - German slang for grouch or stinker
* hosenscheißer - or trouser pooper - German
 slang for coward or scaredy pants.

"Look, Anna," Elizabeth whispered as they made their way quietly through the trees. What is John doing on the other side of the river? He will spoil our surprise if he sees us."

"Yes, but Henry is dozing. Perhaps we can sneak up while John's back is turned," Anna replied as they crept quietly closer to the protruding rock that Henry lay sprawled on with one hand covering his face and the other dangling in the cool river.

All at once, they all heard a frantic splashing and scuffling sound across the river. Henry, jolted out of his doze, sat bolt upright and stared. Anna and Elizabeth watched on in horror from their hiding spot in the trees as two Indians dragged John into the underbrush on the other side of the river, one hand over his mouth, and a knife held out in threat towards Henry.

"STOP! HELP! INDIANS!" Henry heard his voice shout as if it were coming from some distant hill, echoing through his mind. "This wasn't happening. Where were they taking him?" he thought. Then the worst thought of all, "It's my fault!"

Dropping the lunch pails, Anna tore out of her hiding spot, Elizabeth hot on her heels, and was next to Henry in a flash, holding him back from chasing after his friend and his captors.

"No Henry, you can't! They'll kill you or take you as well!" Anna cried. "John needs us to alert the town." She was shaking Henry now, compelling him to calm down and think. "Henry, stop! I mean GO! Go to the Verein* and tell the men there. Elizabeth and I will run home and tell Papa and Mr. Seipp. Now GO!"

Finally, Henry shook himself out of his panic, and he ran. He was only minutes from town, but it seemed like hours, as his bare feet pounded the hot dusty main street, dirt flying from every

Verein Kirche – (Society Church) Headquarters and public building for The Society.

step in his wake, like a horse at a gallop. Soon he was at the Director's office at the Verein compound, shouting and pounding on the door.

"They've taken John! Indians have taken John!" Henry cried out with tears streaming down his face and panic in his eyes. Oh, why did he challenge him? Why didn't they just go home for lunch?

13

Despair

Quickly a search party of men gathered. Anna ran home as fast as she could while Elizabeth followed along with the nearly forgotten lunchpails.

"Papa ... Mama!" She cried as she burst into the house finding Papa mid-bite on a corn cake. "They've taken John! Hurry! I must go tell Mr. Seipp!"

"What? Slow down Anna. Who has taken John?" Papa jerked his head up and replied in alarm, standing up and knocking over the bench he was sitting on.

"Indians! John was across the river. We just saw them as they snatched him and went into the trees next to the river across from Mr. Adams' house. Henry has gone to the Verein to alert the Director." Anna panted, catching her breath.

Papa headed for the door, but paused to pick up his gun. He learned to shoot as promised when they arrived, and Anna thought at this moment it was a very good thing he had.

"Anna, you run over to Mr. Seipp's house. I'll get my horse and be there right away. Then you go to the Verein and tell them we are coming."

Just after Anna darted off, her feet flying, Elizabeth came into the doorway. Papa stepped around her, a worried look on his face as he picked his well-worn hat off its peg near the door and walked out.

"Elizabeth, thank you," Mama sighed, taking the pails. "You best go home. Tell your parents what has happened. Your mother, Anna, and I will go sit with Mrs. Seipp while the men go search.

In front of the Verein, Henry sat sniveling in the heat, dust from the horse's hooves clinging to the tears on his face. Anna and Mama found him there, after the men mounted their horses and galloped away.

"Henry," Mama explained gently, "It's not your fault. Remember, we all, including John's family, chose to move into Indian Territory. Unless we can make peace, we'll always live in danger. We've all heard the warnings from Jim Shaw about the Comanche stealing people, even from other Comanche tribes. Sometimes they keep them and adopt them, and sometimes they ransom them back."

Henry grimaced and retorted angrily, "And sometimes they beat them and make them slaves. Sometimes they kill them, just for fun."

Anna took Henry's hand and offered, "We will pray for him, and for his safety. Jim Shaw will help, wait and see. Don't lose hope yet." But Anna could see, once more, Henry close into himself with anger, guilt, and hatred blinding him to everything and everyone else.

As they walked home to gather some things to take with them, they saw John's house in the distance, pecan trees casting a shadow on the porch, and the figure of a woman sitting with her head in her hands.

"We will get a jar of honey and some corn bread and take it to John's mother. The men may not get back until late, and we will keep her company," Mama pointed out as they entered the gate to their yard. "We must be brave for her sake."

They sat with Mrs. Seipp for over four hours, helping with her chores.

Worry etched her face and fear hung in the air like fog.

Anna, trying to distract everyone, observed, "I just can't get used to the heat. They say the winters will be much milder than in Germany, but we are paying for it now. At least it is cooling now as the sun goes past the trees." But no one was very talkative and soon quiet returned. It was enough to just be silent companions.

They were all sitting, staring down the road, sweat running down their backs, when they saw the men return without John.

While they watched Mr. Seipp and Papa approach on their mounts, Mama, Anna, and the others drifted away to give Mr. and Mrs. Seipp some privacy. With a disappointed look on his dirty, weary face, Papa told the group of comforters, "We were able to track the

Indians for over an hour and know which direction they are headed. Tomorrow we will go see the Delaware and ask if Jim Shaw is around and can help. He will negotiate a ransom, I think."

Looking across the yard, Anna saw John's father leading his mother into the house, her shoulders shaking from sobs of pain. Anna heard her anguished voice float through the air as if John, with his eager open expression, was drifting away as well. "My boy, my sweet boy, I'll never see him again. He is lost, I just know he is."

Days and weeks passed, but still, there was no word from Jim Shaw or the Indian agents who were searching. There was no report on John's whereabouts or even existence. There were so many Comanche bands, each with their own chief and their own ways. Papa often claimed if the Comanche banded together and were organized, they could outnumber all the whites in the state. If that was the case, they may never find John. He could be hundreds of miles away since the Comanche were nomadic and came and went with the buffalo.

Anna knew Henry was miserable without his friend, and this was his newest reason to fear and hate the Wild Ones. "Why won't they just leave us alone," he huffed gloomily, as he went about his chores. He knew some were kind, like Running Deer and Jim Shaw, but he remembered the cruelty they possessed. Every time he saw Schmidt's old gun hanging above their door, he remembered.

14

Home

A month later, on a September day with a hint of fall in the air, Anna's fingers ached as she gripped the handles of the two heavy wooden buckets filled with water she carried to the Seipp's house. Mrs. Seipp depended on her to help with John's chores. Henry did what he could, but now, more than ever, he was needed in the fields to harvest the corn. It was a race against time to harvest enough to see them through the winter.

Her boots kicked at tufts of prairie grass, disturbing the dragon flies, sending them buzzing around her sweating face as she trudged across the path leading to the Seipp's homestead. She rounded the corner to enter the yard when, through the glare of the sun, she spotted three Indians riding into town, their horses kicking up a cloud of dust on the main road leading to the headquarters.

She kept her slow, steady pace, not wanting to spill the water, but watching the small group in the distance.

Anna's thoughts drifted to the storms the day before, with big blustery clouds and thunder. During the howling winds Anna and Henry sat huddled in their cabin, each thinking about their friend. "I wonder where John is right now," Henry grieved. "Is he dry … safe … or even alive?"

"Henry," Anna replied, "when Elizabeth was so sick, we picked a lucky star in the night sky and that helped us make it through Karlshafen and other miseries. The stars in the sky shine over John the same way they shine over you. God took care to put each star in the sky. He will care for John too."

Anna didn't think she had cheered him, but now after the storm cleared and a cool breeze followed, she watched the three riders approach the Verein compound and stop. Her pulse quickened as she thought what this could mean.

Finally, she found a good spot to put down her buckets and ran toward the group, who were now talking to the Director excitedly with their hands. As she approached, she saw Henry was there too, and her heart leapt when she saw one of the riders was Jim Shaw and the other two were Comanche.

"Henry," Anna panted as she came to the rear of the group of men, "Do they have word of John?"

Henry didn't even glance at Anna. Instead, he broke through the small crowd and demanded, pointing at the Indians, "Director! Do they have him? Are they talking about John?"

Henry's father, who was in the crowd with Mr. Seipp, jerked him by his collar away from the men and cautioned with a growl, "Don't interfere, Henry! They have John and are negotiating a ransom. Do you want to cause a problem? Do you want your friend back? If so, stay out of the way and let the Director negotiate."

Henry found Anna at the back of the crowd. Raking his shaking hands through his hair, he turned to Anna, and exploded, "John is alive! He will be ransomed! But how ... HOW ... could the Indians demand payment for someone THEY stole! How can I feel so happy, angry, and ashamed at the same time? They did this evil thing and now they want a reward for it? Justice would demand punishment, not a reward!"

"Henry, I don't know. How are any of us supposed to understand what they do?" Anna felt her face begin to flood with heat, the hope and anger beginning to overwhelm her. Holding a hand up as if to block Henry's anger from washing over her, she pleaded, "But John is alive and will be home soon. Nothing can spoil that. One day ... perhaps one day we will live in peace."

"Peace? Peace? How can peace ever happen if this is what they do?" Henry fumed, throwing his hands in the air, pacing back and forth, kicking up dust.

"Yes, peace!" Anna retorted, turning on him with her hair stuck to the sweat on her face. "Remember, this was their home before it was ours." Taking deep breaths, she continued, "It will be better if we can make a treaty like Papa says. I am as frustrated as you," she implored, "but what good does it do anyone to get angry? You have to look for the good in things, and right now the good is John is coming home!"

Before Henry could reply, Papa approached, lines etched across his tired face, and sighed, "All right, they will exchange John for what they call 'brown water', corn, and 'a beast with horns like a buffalo'." Papa announced, shaking his head. "Mr. Seipp and I will go now and get the coffee and corn from his account at the Society storehouse. You two go quickly and share the news with Mrs. Seipp. She will gladly give up their cow."

They found John's mother sitting on a low stool under a tree in the back of the house, picking pecans out of the dirt and putting them in her apron pocket. Seeing their happy expressions she cried, "You have good news! Is it John?" She stood, pecans falling from her apron as her hands flew to her face and she began to weep with tears of joy.

"Yes! He is coming home! Ransom is being gathered now. They want a cow … we can share some milk from our goats with you," Anna volunteered, knowing how hard it would be for them to lose their only cow.

Mrs. Seipp wiped her hands on her apron, pulled her shoulders back, and consented, "Thank you, Anna dear, we appreciate it. You are good friends to us. I'll get the cow, not a second to waste!"

Elizabeth, hearing the news, ran to meet Anna at the Seipp's house as others gathered as well. She asked, "How will they get the supplies? What will they do?"

Anna replied, "John's father is getting the corn and some coffee from the Verein storehouse. It will be charged against his account, but he'd gladly pay it ten times, I'm sure. Although it will pinch their supplies, we will all help where we can."

As they were putting a harness on the cow, Mr. Seipp strode up to Mrs. Seipp and exclaimed, "I see you've heard the good news. Our boy is coming home!" More gently he added, "Don't worry now, it will all be over soon, and we will be together again."

After all the requested items were gathered and given to the Indians with the assurance John would be returned shortly, Anna, Elizabeth, and Henry sat on a fallen tree near the edge of town. Their chores were forgotten as they anxiously watched the horizon.

The day seemed to stretch on forever, until Anna cried, "Look, I think I see them!" They all stood, shielding their eyes with their hands, and gazing toward a clump of trees on a distant hill.

Fear gripped at their hearts as minutes passed. But soon, to their great relief, they saw Jim Shaw riding slowly towards town with an extra rider on the back of his horse. Henry did not wait, but ran towards them as fast as his legs would carry him.

"John!" Henry cried from a distance, but his friend did not respond. His head drooped forward and rolled side to side in rhythm with each lumbering step the horse took. It tore at Henry's heart. Anxiously, he watched as they approached, the horse picking his way carefully along the trail.

Finally, they were close, and Henry saw John was ghostly thin and badly bruised, one eye swollen shut, and a partially healed scar across his cheek. "John ... it's me, Henry. I've come to welcome you home. Your parents are coming. Look, I see them!" Henry said gently.

With those words, John slowly raised his head and tried mightily to compose himself. He took a shuddering breath and sighed, "Thanks, Henry, for the welcome. It's good to be home."

15

A New Search

Anna yawned and stretched as she walked outside in the cool morning. She saw a faint light beginning to rise in the east, behind the distant hills with oak trees sweeping up their sides, casting long shadows. The days were shorter now, and the January chill was upon them.

Shuddering, Anna remembered last January. Only a year ago, they were in Karlshafen, living in a sand cave shelter in the dunes, with little food but a lot of misery. Looking back, she knew The Society was not prepared for the number of immigrants arriving on ships every week, and Anna felt lucky their family found shelter with at least a small degree of windbreak from the constant gales. She remembered hanging a quilt over the opening for privacy, but it did little to nothing to keep the mosquitoes at bay. They constantly buzzed and bit all night long. She thought of her friend Elizabeth, and how sick she was by the time she arrived in New Braunfels. How she was so lucky as to avoid the coastal diseases plaguing every group of settlers, she did not know. The cave was misery.

She looked over her shoulder at their home now and smiled as she remembered their entire family's effort in building it not long after they arrived. Papa, with Henry's help, cut and smoothed each small tree for the four walls while she and Mama gathered and wove grass together to form a temporary roof, until shingles could be made from the mill. They helped neighbors too. Mr. Seipp and John worked alongside Papa and Henry while making the walls, and they, in turn, helped them. Henry was a good worker and learned quickly, but Anna remembered Mr. Seipp being stern and hard on John, always correcting his errors, barking, "How will you learn if I do not correct you? No, you are doing it wrong again! Pay attention son!" If Anna was honest, in those days John didn't always pay attention. He loved life and all of nature and was often distracted by the smallest creature clinging to the side of a tree. That was before the Indians ... his good humor had since returned, but he was more watchful and careful than before.

About a month after his return, when she and Mama were resting under a tree watching John crouch to catch a lizard, Mama mentioned, "I think John perhaps would make a good naturalist. I hope to see him write a book about the wildlife of the Texas frontier."

Anna thought about this and replied, "Yes! What a grand idea! He could include bears, panthers, jaguars, buffalo, deer and eagles." Henry, overhearing, laughed and said, "I think he needs to include those horrible rattlesnakes, and horned lizards and scorpions," as he snuck up behind Anna and ran his fingers up her back. Anna let out a shriek, and warned, "One of these days, Henry! One of these days!"

In the eight months since they arrived, the mill never did come into being. But, luckily for them, the grass roof proved to be remarkably waterproof. Thank goodness there were so few mosquitoes in the hill country compared to the coast.

Anna shook her head sadly as she remembered the disappointment the whole town felt after the months passed with no millstone arriving. She knew her papa would have plenty of work after it arrived. For now though, all the houses were like theirs - rough logs with thatched roofs and only a few bare windows. The windows were covered with oiled animal hide since there was no glass, or for that matter, no wood trim with which to frame them. There were plenty of rocks, though, and they laid a good hearth for a fireplace. Their home was warm enough when the wind wasn't blowing too hard. Their floor was packed dirt now, but one day it would be made of wood planks from the mill.

Henry emerged from the house, joining Anna as she gazed at the horizon, shaking the sleep from his head like a dog and shaking out his shirt to check for scorpions. They liked to crawl into the sleeves as it hung on its peg at night. A month earlier he was stung by one and learned quickly to be careful when dressing. Henry was now a full head taller than Anna having grown nearly five inches in the last few months. The healthy air and hard work was good for both of them, and they were growing stronger each day in spite of the lack of vegetables Mama said were so important.

They worked hard alongside their parents, and Papa kept his word. Over time, he and Henry both learned to shoot, practicing often and competing in shooting clubs as more and more immigrants arrived. Henry, it seems, was a natural, and was known around town for his ability to hit a squirrel in a tree from quite a distance. There were times when squirrel meat was the only meat at hand, and they were grateful for Henry's ability to provide it. Today, the morning sky was a brilliant pink, with only a few low-lying clouds. It was cold, but the sun would warm them as they worked, feeding the few chickens and goats they acquired since arriving last May.

The two goats were a gift for their birthdays, which were both in July. When Papa led the noisy young goats into the yard, they immediately started dreaming of the milk and cheese they would be tasting one day! Anna named them Millie and Ella, after some friends in Germany, and they both doted upon them every day, petting and playing with them in their free time.

"Well, let's get started," Henry commented, stifling a yawn, and bending down to pick up their pail. They opened the door to the chicken coop, made out of long thin sticks and attached to the jam of the door with leather straps. Chickens fluttered and clucked as they reached under each one to check for eggs, being careful to look for snakes first.

"Henry," Anna asked, glancing around the yard, "have you seen Ella and Millie? They are usually trying to eat my sweater by now."

"You know what? I haven't. How odd! I wonder where they are?" Henry replied, craning his neck to look out the coop door.

With their pail full, they shooed the chickens out of the coop to graze in the dooryard. Walking around the small house, they called, "Millie … Ella!" louder and louder with growing concern. Mama came out of the house with a quizzical look, asking, "What is wrong? Where are Ella and Millie?"

"I'm not sure Mama," Henry replied, "but I think Anna and I need to go into the forest and look for them. It's not like them to go far, and they may have gotten lost." With a grin, he added, "I don't think the Director will fire the cannon so they can find their way home. It will have to be all our doing to bring them back to safety."

Over the summer, a cannon arrived in one of the wagon trains, and the Director would sometimes fire it when someone was reported missing. The forest was very thick, and it was easy to lose your way. The cannon served as their homing signal; their beacon in a sea of trees.

"Oh Henry, don't tease! You know ... the Indians ..." Mama trailed off, worried.

But ignoring Mama, Henry continued, "But perhaps he *would* fire the cannon for Millie and Ella. Afterall, he fired it for Mr. Adams last week, and he is deaf!"

Anna suppressed a giggle, unable to resist her brother's good-natured humor, but she also knew Mama was right. The Wild Ones were a constant threat. But still, she worried about their prized goats. They needed the milk and so did John and his family. She would be distraught if anything were to happen to them.

Anna added, "Mama, Henry is right. I do think we need to go find them. They may have just decided to forage for buried acorns under the big oaks. We will be quick and will look out for each other."

Reluctantly, Mama agreed, but said, "Papa, I think, would want you to take the gun. He won't be back from Austin until tomorrow, and Henry, you know how to handle it. You will do well to remember what happened to John." Mama continued, "It can happen so fast...."

Henry and Anna remembered well what happened to John. They would need to be very careful, but they were going on a rescue mission.

16

The Rescue

Henry and Anna gathered their supplies. Henry grabbed the gun and two ropes that hung in coils on a hook along the backside of the chicken coop. Anna stuffed her pockets with dried corn to coax the goats along when they became stubborn.

Anna, waiting outside and stomping the hard ground, called to Henry, "Are you ready yet? It's already midmorning. If we don't go now, we may never find them. What are you doing?"

Henry poked his shaggy head out the window and said, "I'm coming, Anna. You can't expect me to go without breakfast. I'm a growing man and have to eat. Don't worry, I grabbed you a boiled egg to eat on the way."

Anna sighed and said, "Henry you are just like the goats, distracted by the possibility of food. Now can we please go before you need to stop for lunch?"

They set off at a brisk pace, skirting the communal cornfield, and heading for the woods. There was a thicket of oaks with especially large acorns Henry knew would be a temptation to the goats.

It took about an hour of walking to get to the spot, and as they walked, they talked about the picnic on the upcoming Sunday afternoon and which of their new friends they most hoped would be there.

"I hope that John will come on Sunday." Henry said, "I want him to teach me to whistle through my teeth." Nudging Anna he added, "Perhaps you should learn too, then you can call your goats home when you are an old lady. You can be the one everyone calls 'the old goat lady that lives at the end of town'."

Anna nudged him back, and said, "Oh Henry, I'm sorry, but you are confused. I'll be the one ..." she broke off as they stepped through a leafy barrier and into a small clearing by a fallen oak – a clearing with two Indians squatting around a small fire.

Anna stopped short and grabbed Henry's arm, pointing to the two Comanche turning sticks with meat on them as flames rose and licked at the dripping meat. Anna could hear the sizzle of fat as it melted off the meat and dripped into the fire.

Ella and Millie were nowhere to be seen, thank goodness. With her eyes, Anna motioned for them to back up into the leafy protection of the woods. Quietly, oh so quietly, they slowly stepped backwards, through the opening in the brush through which they had just come. The ground was covered with rotting winter leaves and moss, making their escape a quiet one, but suddenly, an arrow hit the tree next to Henry with a thunk. They both stared at the arrow as it quivered, its tail feathers hypnotizing them.

Panic rising, Henry blurted, "Run Anna! Use the trees for cover!" and they ran like the wind. The huge oaks were their only defense, since Henry did not have time to load and fire the gun. He wasn't sure he could fire it at another living person anyway. Swerving in and out, in and out, they dodged and ran, looking for all the world like a pair of skitter bugs on water. Another arrow missed Anna by inches as she ran, her legs moving fast and her jaw clenched.

She seemed to notice every sound of the woods and every pulse of blood pumping through her veins. She ran as fast as a rabbit fleeing a fox and felt like she could run like this forever, even with the winter branches clawing at her skirts and tearing bloody stripes on her arms and legs.

She heard a yelp of fear as another arrow missed Henry, but she didn't slow. "Keep going!" she called to Henry, as they raced on through the trees. Then, with the sound of the woods as part of her now, she became aware of a change. There were only two pairs of running feet and no more thwacks of arrows hitting the trees.

She ran on for another few minutes with Henry right behind her before she allowed her pace to slow. Calling to Henry, she panted, "I think we've lost them. I think he's gone back for his breakfast, but just in case, how about you be ready with that gun if he decides to come back."

Henry gasped for breath like a fish on the bank of the river, bent over and vomited. Then, hands shaking, he loaded and primed the gun and leaned against a tree to rest, trying to stop the pounding in his ears and chest.

Anna sank to the floor of the woods, her knees pulled up and her arms resting on them, a pillow for her head. She sat breathing deeply, trying to stop the shaky feeling in her legs and to not think about how death had just come looking for them.

Finally, after what must have been a long time, Anna said, "Henry, oh Henry. What would Mama have done if we'd been killed or taken by the Indians? She'd kill us!"

Henry, feeling a little better, and trying to distract Anna, said with a small grin, "Well, Anna. I'm glad that didn't happen because it would be terrible to be killed twice, once by the Indians and once by Mama!"

Anna puffed a sound of disgust, and sighed, "Oh Henry, you are impossible," but began to quietly laugh. Unable to help themselves, they both laughed until tears filled their eyes.

17

Lost

Wiping her face with her sleeve and taking deep breaths, Anna began to look around at the thick clusters of bare-branched oaks and the rise of a hill in the distance, just beyond a small valley. Next to her, there was a rocky ledge just higher than her shoulder with a trickle of water moistening its rough face making the ground below it boggy. It smelled like springtime in spite of the bare trees. Delicate ferns grew out of the moist soil and clung to the sides of the outcropping. She turned and asked, "Henry … where are we? I don't recognize it. I think I'd recognize this place if I'd seen it before."

Henry's smile faded as he too looked around with concern. He responded, "No, I don't either. It's a pretty spot. I think I'd remember it if I'd been here before. Let's get to a clearing so I can see the sun and get my bearings."

They walked quietly, aware of all the sights and sounds around them, keeping alert for the Indians and for Ella and Millie. "Oh, where are those goats," Anna thought as she walked. "They must be lost and frightened, wanting their home by now. I hope a panther or jaguar* hasn't gotten them!"

As they entered a clearing and saw the sun was lower in the sky than they expected, Henry said, "It gets dark early in January. Look, the sun is past noon.

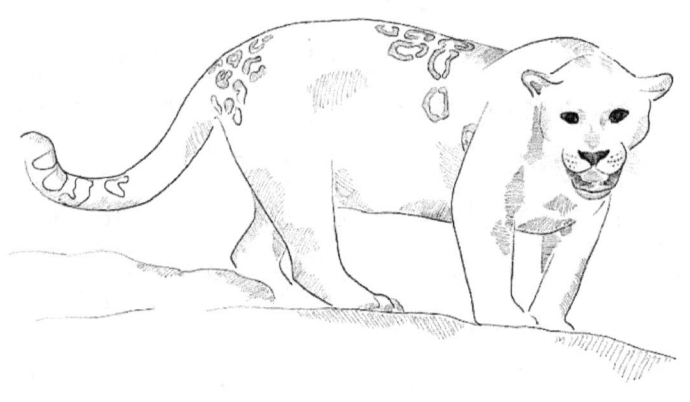

Jaguars - During the 1800s, Texas was the jaguar's northernmost territory, and the last known jaguar was killed in Texas in 1940. During this time in Fredericksburg, there were many jaguars and they were the largest cat in Texas. The second largest is the panther, who still lives in Texas today.

We'd better get a move on and find our wayward friends, or it will be bad for all of us." Pointing towards a not-too-distant hill, Henry suggested, "Let's climb that rise, it will offer us a better view and perhaps we can see smoke from the town. Listen closely as we go."

It was a long walk and Anna ignored her growing hunger and the sting of the scratches and cuts on her arms, legs, and face, filled now with dirt and sweat. Crossing the clearing, Anna tried to think only of the beauty of the land, even in the winter, with its tall, swaying grass which grew in every open space, towering oaks, pecan trees heavy with nuts, and the beautiful rock outcroppings which seemed to sprout right out of the earth.

She remembered how in the summer, there were wildflowers ... so many wildflowers. Her thoughts wandered as she remembered picking them every day and giving posies to Mama. One of her favorites had slender, graceful, bright purple petals that hung onto a bristly center the size of a goat's eye. The petals delicately hung like a swooning princess from her fairy tales in the arms of her beloved. Another was a completely yellow daisy, as bright as the noonday sun. Once, she gathered a posy and, finding her mother in the street talking to a group of people, handed it to her. One of the men in the group, an Indian agent, turned and commented, "That is quite a beautiful bunch of flowers you have there young lady. Did you know the Indians use them medicinally? The purple ones make a curative tea, and the yellow ones they say can cure eye problems. You know, we'd be wise to remember there are actually a lot of things we can learn from the Wild Ones. Gather and dry those flowers over the summer, and you will be prepared for the winter illnesses."

Anna and Mama heeded his advice and their kitchen shelf was lined with a store of dried herbs. Now, the flowers were sleeping for the winter. Some days, she wished she could sleep for the winter too, like the bears and the flowers. Some days were bitterly cold and dreary, but nothing like their winters in Germany. Although their house in Germany was a proper one with a sturdy roof, that roof would have been covered with snow almost all winter. She nearly froze just walking to school in Germany.

Here, in her new home, she thought as she walked, the winters seemed almost balmy in comparison.

There were cold days for sure, but they never lasted too long. It would be a bundle up day one day and a shawl day the next. Often there were days with temperatures of winter, spring, and summer all in one day! The morning on any given day might start with a blazing sun strong enough to cause a sweat, and by lunchtime, there would be blustering, whipping winds and freezing temperatures. Then, the very next day it would be warm and sunny again. It was as if the Texas sun was too strong to let winter take hold more than a day or two. She was relieved that today turned out to be a light shawl day, warm in the sun, a slight chill in the shade.

As they entered the woods on the far side of the clearing, they both heard a faint bleating in the distance. Exchanging a hopeful glance, they headed in that direction. With an excited laugh, Henry exclaimed, "We may have found our greedy goats! Shall we lecture them all the way home, as Mama would do to us? Perhaps we should have them write a note of apology. Ah well, there is nothing to write with in Fredericksburg anyway, no paper or ink so I guess we'll have to forgive them."

Having no writing materials was a subject of much discussion in their house. Henry rejoiced in it since that meant no writing in school. Anna, however, mourned the loss of writing. She wanted to draw and write stories. She missed her school in Germany. Here, they recently started having occasional small gatherings, organized by the parents, to try to keep up their education, but the children were needed at home or in the fields most of the time. When they could, though, they went to one house or another to gather and hear stories of famous Germans – the great composers, artists, architects and scientists. Sometimes they would learn about practical things, like farming, but also what seemed to them to be impractical, like reciting math facts and spelling words.

Continuing their search, they hurried towards the growing sounds of bleating goats, and as they rounded a tight cluster of trees, there they were, happily munching on the acorns uprooted from the ground. Anna cried out, "Oh Ella! Millie! How glad I am to see you two foolish goats! What made you run away? How could you do this to us?"

With a happy grin of relief, Henry replied, "They decided they were going to go to Austin! They heard there was a trail that needed to be cleared and determined that their stomachs were the perfect ones to do it, one acorn at a time!"

Anna replied, "Well, I'm glad we've found them. Come on Henry, let's go home. Mama is going to be worried to death!" She grabbed the rope from over her shoulder and quickly made a lead rope for Millie while Henry made one for Ella.

While he worked, Henry said, "Sorry old girl. Your fun is over. Time to go home and take care of the family." And with that, he and Anna led them through the surrounding trees and into a clearing, always watching for Indians and coaxing the goats along with the corn when they tried to stop and nibble a tasty root or acorn.

The goats, which were purchased by The Society and distributed to the citizens of Fredericksburg as allotted by their investments, were an enormous blessing to the health of the community. Even though the Schupp family managed to stay healthy so far, many became ill from scurvy and malnutrition. Their diet was mainly meat, corn, and coffee. Anna's family also had eggs and the dried flowers which Mama ground and put into tea. She shared what she could, but there were so many coming into town every week!

Seeing Anna's expression, Henry asked, "Why the long face? We have our friends, and we are headed home! We shall be home for dinner! Come on now, let's go." Then, looking around, said, "The rise is just there, through these trees. Let's see if we can find the town from there," and they walked on, with new purpose, even though it was far and they were both hungry and tired.

When they crested the rise, Henry stood, mouth open, and stared at the horizon. Then he deflated like a balloon. His shoulders drooped and his chin fell to his chest. Not looking at Anna, he said in a flat tone, "We are lost. It's late and we are lost."

Anna could see how low the sun was on the horizon and knew the day was short. She went to Henry, determined, and put both hands on his shoulders. "Henry," she said, "I'm not going to be Little Red Riding Hood tonight. Do you hear me? Not tonight! We will make it home and we will not get eaten by a panther, jaguar, OR wolf. Think Henry! Look, the sun can be our guide. If it is setting over there," she continued, pointing to the west, "then we need to go that way," she finished, pointing to the east. "Look, there is another hill over there. Let's make it that far. If we still see nothing, we can find a place to camp."

"Alright, we can try that," Henry said, trying to ignore the tightening in his stomach. He pulled and yanked on Ella's lead rope and hurried down the hill in the direction Anna pointed out.

Millie, not wanting to be left behind, pulled Anna along, slipping and sliding through the dead leaves. As Anna slid down the hill, struggling to keep her footing, she saw Henry tumble over a root and fall face first into a clump of dried leaves, dropping the gun and rope in the process.

Standing, Henry tottered slightly as he shook his head. Finally, the tension was too much, and Anna laughed out loud. She teased, "You look like you just ate our Oma's* sauerkraut! But oh! That makes my mouth water.

*Oma - German for "grandmother"

I do hope we have cabbage in our garden next summer. I miss sauerkraut and Mama says it will be so good for everyone."

Henry picked up the gun and rope, shaking his head slowly at Anna, and said, "I think you've lost it, sister. Laughing when your brother is dying," but he hid a smile as he walked.

They were just leaving the woods and heading down a sloping hill, picking their way through the hidden rocks buried beneath the winter leaves and fallen oak trees, when they froze, excitement crossing their weary faces.

"Oh Henry, did you hear that?" Anna exclaimed. "It was the cannon! They are firing it for us! We are saved!"

Not wasting a second, Henry said, "Come on! Get a move on Ella! We are headed home for supper! Move it now, or you'll be our supper!" And they both turned towards the sound and hurried in that direction, not caring about the sinking sun, the branches that whipped

at their faces and hands, or the growing chill of the oncoming night.

As Fredericksburg came into sight, Anna said with relief, "Just think, Henry, what started this morning as a rescue mission ended in our own rescue by The Society's cannon. At least we have Millie and Ella returning home with us. Mama may never let us out of her sight again."

18

An Expedition

A week later, Anna and Henry were gathered in John's house, along with seven other children their age, reciting the quote by the famous German poet, Johann Wolfgang von Goethe, "Knowing is not enough; we must apply. Willing is not enough; we must do," when the door flew open and John's father, Mr. Seipp, burst in and exclaimed, "Meusebach is determined! We are going into Comanche Territory!" Then looking around at the children, his eyes softened as he said, "Ah, you are studying Goethe I see. Well, boys and girls, 'willing is not enough', we won't have peace with the Indians until we make it happen. We will begin preparations tomorrow." And with that, he grinned broadly and gave a big whoop.

Anna and Henry looked around open-mouthed, then Henry jumped up and ran out, Anna hot on his heels. They ran home and screeched to a halt just before crashing straight into Mr. Meusebach as he was leaving. "Whoa there, son, what's the rush?"

"Hello Mr. Meusebach, sir. It's so nice to see you again. I've just heard you are forming an expedition into Comanche Territory to make a peace treaty. I've come to talk to Papa about it. Is he going with you? May I go as well?"

Henry blurted before he could stop himself.

Mr. Meusebach shook his head and grinned at Henry, saying, "Well son, as much as I admire your courage and your honest eagerness to join in, I think your father will need you at home, to hunt and watch after your sister and mother. Your father has indeed agreed to go with us and will be a valuable asset to the group. Now run on in and see what you can do to help him gather the supplies he will need for the trip."

Henry and Anna said their goodbyes to Mr. Meusebach and found Mama and Papa in the house in serious conversation. "Don't worry, Christine, Meusebach is no fool. He is shrewd and will deal fairly with the Indians. We will be home before you know it with a peace treaty in hand," Papa was saying as Mama kept her nerves down by straightening the jars on the shelves which held the ground herbs for their tea. "There is nothing greater I can do than help forge a peace with the wild ones, so we can stop living in fear for our lives while we go about our daily chores. Why just yesterday, two Indians on horseback chased Herr Keller and his son while they were out looking for their lost cow. But they were riding swift horses and were quick thinking enough to throw out the sausages from their saddlebags, or they may not be with us today. The Indians paused long enough to pick up the sausages, and they got away. I cannot overemphasize how important this is!"

Mama replied, "I know William, I know … it's just you will be gone for so long, and what if the Indians come here while you are gone?"

"The Director will be here, and there will be men enough to carry on with the work. We will be back before spring planting. Don't worry, Christine. It must be done," Papa said as he gently pulled Mama into a hug.

A week later, on a cold January day, Papa and thirty-nine other men were ready to go. The wagons were loaded with gifts for the Indians – peace offerings, including the special beads the Indians were so fond of that Mr. Meusebach made for the occasion – as well as food, supplies and ammunition. Anna, Henry, and Mama bravely joined the other townspeople as they waved the group off with much shouting of goodwill and good wishes. John was there as well and teased Anna, "Now, Henry is the man of the house! And you will be gathering eggs all by yourself. Be sure to watch out for those snakes and...."

"Nope! Oh no she won't," Henry interrupted with a wink to his sister, "Do you think those chickens will give eggs without me around? They need my handsome face to inspire them!"

Anna knew Henry would not leave her to do all the chores, even if it meant more work for him. He was finally becoming a good man, like Papa, and she was glad. As she walked back to their little house, down the muddy road, she knew they were a family, and they would be okay.

The weeks moved on, and their lives evolved into a new routine, without Papa around. Henry would hunt in the afternoons, sometimes with John, and sometimes with Anna. He never went alone, though, because there was still the threat of Indians. One afternoon, as Anna and Elizabeth were stirring the big laundry pot on the fire, Henry and John came tearing down the road panting, "Indians are coming! We saw them as they came around the hill. We were up on the ridge and saw them below us. We came as fast as we could, but they are approaching now!" The town was in an instant uproar. Were the Indians here now when they knew the expedition was gone, so they could plunder the town and steal their horses?

Anna, not wanting to be left alone, hurried with Henry down the road behind the Director. Quickly, the Director relaxed and announced to the milling groups, "It's all right. Look, he's brought his women and children with him. He hasn't come to fight. Let's go out and see what he wants." Looking behind him at Anna and Henry, he continued, "You two, come along with me, and he will see we mean no harm."

Anna and Henry fell in step with the Director and a few others to meet the old chief. His wrinkled face and thin body did not look to Anna like the face of a war chief until she looked into his eyes, where she saw wisdom and cunning. Through an interpreter, Chief Old Owl asked, "Why do your men go into Comanche hunting grounds? Do they wish to war with the Comanche? I have been watching them for weeks as they travel deeper and deeper into our territory."

The Director responded with an emphatic, "No! We are a peaceful people and we go to give gifts and make peace treaties with all your Comanche brothers. We welcome you to our town and invite you to stay the night with us. We have space in a building right here, and would be honored for you to stay and eat with us."

Anna, Henry, and John looked with fascination at the Indians. They saw the more civilized Delaware tribe many times before they left for better hunting ground when it turned cold, but they never dared to get so close to a Comanche.

As Elizabeth caught up with Anna, she said, "Look how straight and proud they stand. And look, they don't have any hair. Do you think they shave it?"

Anna hid a smile as her friend stared at the Indians who were almost completely bare of any hair except for their two long braids with eagle's feathers and beads woven into them. Their bare chests looked like old leather, but strong and muscular, and their noses were long with high strong cheekbones. To Anna, they looked very wild.

"They are staying the night!" Anna told Elizabeth as they left the crowd of onlookers and hurried home to tell the news to their mothers. "Before you found me, I heard the Director invite them to eat and stay in the guest house. Just think, Comanches right here in town!"

As the Indians settled in for dinner, the boys wandered back to their homes for their own meal. While they were eating the stew Mama prepared with squirrel meat, onions, and corn, Anna asked, "Do you think we are safe from the Indians? Can you believe how many there are? I'm glad our house is far away from where they are camping. Do you think they will stay awhile? Do you think they are going to find the expedition...."

Mama interrupted, "Goodness Anna, so many questions. I think we are quite safe, but just the same, bring Millie and Ella to the front of the house for the night. I'd hate to lose them again."

After dinner, Anna secured the goats to the front by a short lead rope and put a bucket of water within reach. She then joined Mama and Henry outside on some stumps they used for stools and listened. They could hear the warriors in the distance, at their camp outside of the town. They knew Old Owl and some of his women were settling into the small building with two rooms off an open breezeway. One room was the pharmacy and the other was an empty room sometimes used to house travelers passing through.

Mama looked towards town, bathed in the moonlight, and sighed deeply. "I hope your father is well, and all the men with him."

"He is Mama! From the interpreter, we know where they are, and they are safe. Even Old Owl wants peace!" Anna sighed as her body relaxed against the rough logs of the house.

Henry replied, "They want peace right now, but can we trust them? Their peace may depend on what they can get from us. I saw the Director gathering gifts for them from the town's supplies."

Mama agreed, "Yes, you're right, Henry. The Director is giving gifts to them from the town's supplies, but, if it brings us peace, it is well worth it. This living in constant fear isn't good for the soul. It will take time to earn their trust. Since Old Owl brought his family, I hope it means he desires peace." Mama continued adjusting the stump so she could lean against the side of the house and rest her head on the curve of a log. "We will see what the morning brings. Now you two, let's settle in for the night. It's getting cold outside.

19

A Cry of Alarm

The three went inside and Anna and Henry pulled out the thin pallet they shared which served as their mattress. It was rough spun cotton stuffed with corn husks and was kept under their parent's bed on a trundle during the day. Mama and Papa's bed was small with ropes to hold their corn husk mattress off the ground. Mama worked to keep the ropes tight with the bed wrench and to keep the bugs out of their mattresses.

As soon as they settled in, Henry rolled over and was fast asleep, but Anna lay awake for an hour, listening to the distant sounds and thinking about their father, so far away. It was many hours later that she stirred and noticed Henry wasn't in bed. She squinted in the darkness but did not see him anywhere. She whispered, "Henry, where are you?" There was no reply.

Just then, there was a distant, but distinct cry of alarm, followed by noises of confused struggling and other cries of alarm from outside of town, where the Indians were camped.

"Oh Henry, where are you ...?" Anna muttered under her breath as she rose off the floor. Anna woke her mother saying, "Mama, wake up! Something is going on! Henry's is not here, and ..."

She didn't get out another word, before her mother was up and out the door, peering into the darkness. The full moon was low over the trees, and the light from it was fainter than before. There were dark shadows in the distance, and someone was running towards them, in the dark; an indistinct blur, heading straight for them. They shrank into the shadows and watched the figure approach, helpless to defend themselves.

When the shadowy figure entered their gate, Anna bravely wrapped her fingers around a walking stick propped by the door, ready to defend herself and Mama any way she could. She slowly raised the makeshift weapon, and then with a gasp, released it in relief. Henry came out of the shadows, and Anna cried, "Henry Schupp! I nearly clubbed you! Where have you been and what in the world is going on?"

Henry, seeing them both, hesitated only slightly, and then grinned, "You aren't going to believe it! I heard noises so I went to investigate. It was a militia group from New Braunfels coming into town in the middle of the

night. I followed them to see what was going on. They went into the same house that Old Owl was in – into the other room, the one they usually stay in on the south side. Anyway, Old Owl ... he saw the men and he came out of the house like a shot out of the cannon, his women right behind him. Mama, he wasn't wearing his clothes! He left so fast, he didn't take time to dress! He and all his warriors have fled in the night! Oh, you should have seen the commotion. Oh man! You should have seen him running down the road, I nearly died! The militiamen were totally unaware the Comanche chief was in the next room. They stood there in the open doorway, scratching their heads in wonder. This will be a story to tell!"

Mama, covering her smile with her hand, said reproachfully, "Henry, it isn't kind to laugh at another man's misfortune. How dreadfully frightened Old Owl must have been, after what happened in San Antonio at the Council House. No wonder he doesn't trust us. He thinks all white people are the same. I'm sure the Director will send someone tomorrow to straighten all this out.

Now, come on inside and try to go back to sleep. Oh my, what a night!"

Anna, poking Henry in the side, said, "You are lucky I didn't club you. Next time take me with you!"

"Sorry, sis," Henry said, as he moved past her and tugged her braid, but this time she was fast and swatted his arm quickly. He turned and bowed, acknowledging her quickness and grinned. He knew she wouldn't stay mad at him.

The next day, Henry was at the Director's office early, wanting to see what was going on. The Director, seeing Henry said, "How would you like to join the group? I need you to go with some men and an interpreter to make peace with Old Owl."

Henry proudly joined the group of men. They returned Old Owl's clothes and other belongings and sent him on his way with good wishes for peace and trust. News spread around town that all was well, and surely they would have peace with the Indians soon.

That afternoon, Henry was helping Anna with some chores and Anna was peppering him with questions. "Why couldn't I go? I'm brave too."

Henry admitted a little sheepishly to Anna, "Old Owl – he said he knew now they meant no harm since they sent a child with them. I thought the Director wanted me to go because I was a man, but now I know he thinks of me only as a boy...."

Anna replied kindly but with a glint in her eye, "Don't worry Henry, one day you will be as big and strong as Papa, and then I can sit around all day and watch you do all the work."

Grinning again, Henry flicked Anna's braid and took off toward the chicken coop and chores.

After dinner that night, they once again were sitting on the stump stools, leaning against the side of the house. Anna said, "What an adventure! What a day!"

Mama sighed and added, "Yes, we've made new friends and that friendship may save us our lives. God is good to us, children, and He has helped us forgive wrongs and receive forgiveness. Let us pray tonight that the men in the expedition are receiving the same grace."

In the weeks that followed and as the weather turned warmer, Anna and Henry worked on preparing their garden, a small plot just beyond the fence with rich and fertile soil. They worked with their hands and the small tools to remove rocks, pull weeds, and turn the rich soil. As they worked, they watched for snakes and spiders that liked to hide under the cool rocks. They would have vegetables this summer, and it would be from their hard work and diligence. They worked hard every day except Sunday. On that day, they dressed in their best clothes and joined the town for church and social time. It was the day they most looked forward to, in spite of having to dress up. It would be their time to laugh with friends, play, and tell stories.

One Sunday afternoon when Anna and Henry were sitting under the shade of an oak tree with their friends, they heard a commotion in the distance. As they straightened up and stretched their necks to see what it was, they saw on the horizon a trail of men on horseback and some wagons further back. With a shout of joy they jumped up and exclaimed, "They're home! They've come back!" And soon the whole town was alive with excitement. They were shouting and running with the rest of the town to greet the weary travelers, who were rewarded with cheers when word was passed of their success.

Papa, spying Mama and the children, climbed off his horse and was at once engulfed in hugs. He exclaimed, "Henry, Anna, how tall you both have grown in only three months! You will be as tall as Mama and me soon! Oh, the stories I have to tell you! We made it all the way to San Saba. We went as far as the San Saba Fort and surveyed the land within the Fisher-Miller Grant area. It was spooky to see only the remains of the fort abandoned so long ago by the

Spaniards. Meusebach has made a treaty with the Comanche, and we have peace with the Indians! We met with Santa Anna as well as Old Owl and Buffalo Hump, all the great Comanche chiefs. They said we were different from the Americans, more straightforward and less reserved, and they called Meusebach, with his red hair and beard, a 'great chief of the sun'! We may not understand their ways, but they have families and want peace just as we do. Wait until I tell you about their appetites! And how the littlest Comanche can ride almost before they can walk! And the honey tree we found." And with that, they headed towards home, sure to be rewarded with tales and adventures.

As Anna walked by her parents' side, she knew that life was truly an adventure. Like Goethe, she knew that willing wasn't enough, you had to DO. To make a home, there were just things you had to do, and she thanked her lucky star God blessed her with Texas as her home.

The End

Acknowledgements

I want to thank Besty Wagner who took me under her wing and always had a positive outlook. Since the day I met her at a book signing of her book, Spirit of Gonzales, she has done nothing but encourage me. I also want to thank Evelyn Weinheimer from the Gillespie County Historical Society and Pioneer Museum in Fredericksburg for her willingness to advise me. My primary source was Robert Penniger's *Fredericksburg, Texas ... The First Fifty Years* originally written in German and printed by my great-grandfather, Arwed Hillman, in 1896. It is filled with first-hand accounts of the first 50 years of Fredericksburg, passing on the stories of all the brave men, women, and children who endured the long journey across Texas and made Fredericksburg their home.

Historical Background

So many brave people have shaped the state of Texas over the years. They carved out a new beginning, facing dangers from people as well as nature. Men, women, and children who emigrated from Germany are among these courageous people. During the time of Stephen F. Austin's land grants and the Texas War for Independence, there were some German immigrants in Texas, such as Friederich Ernst and Charles Fordtran, who founded the town of Industry. The majority of Germans, however, arrived in a wave of emigration during the time period of May 1845 – July of 1847, which turned out to be a very busy time in the history of Texas!

While Texas was still a Republic, the city of New Braunfels was founded in March of 1845 as a way station for German immigrants traveling to the Fisher-Miller Land Grant past the Llano River. Texas was annexed as a state on December 29, 1845, and the War with Mexico began in April of 1846. In the middle of all this, The Adelsverein, or The Society for the Immigration of German Citizens, helped Germans start a new life in Texas. The Society, as it was called, had purchased the land grant, deep in Comanche Territory, and planned to settle families there. Why did all these people want to leave Germany and try their luck in the wild Comanche Territory? In Germany, people were constantly struggling with overcrowding, poverty, and political problems. As a result, a total of 5,257 people decided to try their luck in

Texas. Sadly, many died along the trip and some settled in towns along the way, but most ended up in the Texas Hill Country.

Unfortunately, as the bulk of the Germans arrived by ship on the coast of Texas, the War with Mexico had just begun, and every extra man, horse,

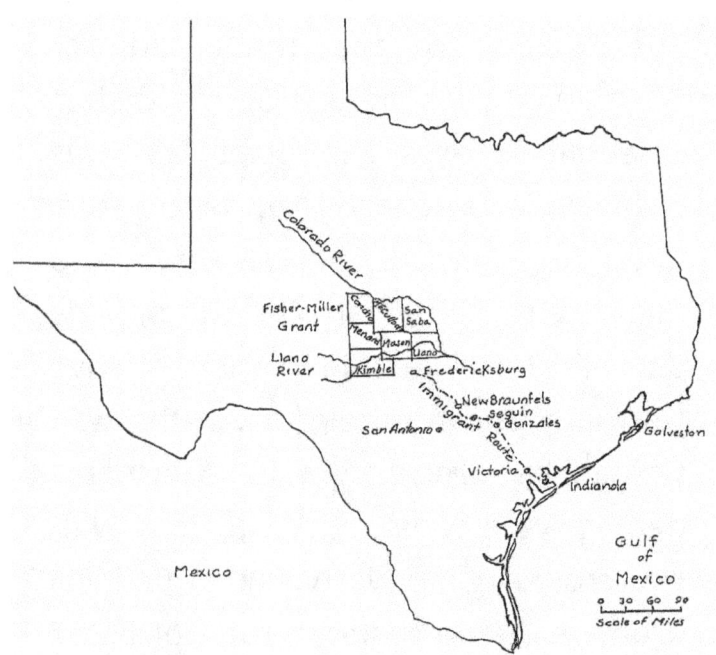

wagon and soldier were occupied with the war. Before May of 1845, few white men, and no white families had dared to travel so far into Comanche Territory. Many Americans called the Germans foolhardy for trying such a thing. However, the Germans were able to do something no one else had been able to do in Texas history. They created a lasting peace with the Comanche, the fiercest of all the Texas Native American people groups.

The Penateka Comanche, who occupied the Balcones Escarpment and the San Saba River region, respected the Germans and had confidence in them to keep their word, mostly due to the leadership skills of John Meusebach, who was Commissioner General of the Society. He was honest and consistent in his treatment of the Native

Americans, and they appreciated this about him.

An excerpt from his speech during the peace negotiation follows:

> "My brother speaks of a division between the red and the pale faces. I do not scorn the red brothers because they have a darker color, and do not regard the whites as noble because they are lighter in color. If our great Father and President wishes to draw a line of distinction, let him do so. We shall not see the distinction because we are brothers and wish to live together as brothers."

The German immigrants were hard-working, diligent, and faithful people, and seventeen percent of Texans today can trace their roots to German ancestors.

For more information and resources for teachers and book clubs please go to susanthomasbooks.com. Also follow Susan Thomas Books on social media @susanthomasbooks.

www.ingramcontent.com/pod-product-compliance
Lightning Source LLC
Chambersburg PA
CBHW060317260626
47160CB00007B/2645